Kita

and the
Astral Awakening

Jeff Hill

Copyright 2020 Jeff Hill

No part of this publication may be reproduced or transmitted in any form or by any means, electronic or mechanical, including photography, recording, or any information storage and retrieval system without prior written consent from the publisher and author except for the purpose of quotes for reviews. No part of this book may be uploaded without the permission of the publisher and author, nor be otherwise circulated in any form of binding, cover other that that in which it is originally published.

This is a work of fiction. Any resemblance to persons, living or dead, or actual events or locales is coincidental. The characters and names are products of the author's imagination and used fictitiously.

The publisher and author acknowledge the trademark status and trademark ownership of all trademarks, service marks and word marks mentioned in this book.

Dedication

*To Tiziana and Lillian
My favorite girl superheroes.*

Contents

Prologue 1
Chapter 1: Trips to the Zoo 3
Chapter 2: Cardiac Arrest 9
Chapter 3: The Champion 15
Chapter 4: Elliot Makes the News 23
Chapter 5: Amanda Griffith 28
Chapter 6: Camera Angles 38
Chapter 7: The Interview 45
Chapter 8: Marlboro Man 56
Chapter 9: A Baby in a Box 63
Chapter 10: Thirteen Candles and a Silo 69
Chapter 11: The Preserve 76
Chapter 12: First Contact 81
Chapter 13: The Astral 88
Chapter 14: Evelyn and Ja'el 94
Chapter 15: Compelling Video 107
Chapter 16: 48K 111
Chapter 17: Bayne 117
Chapter 18: The Walk Home 124
Chapter 19: Neighbors 129
Chapter 20: Ile Brouillard 136
Chapter 21: Antiquities and Alphabets 141
Chapter 22: Granddaughter 150
Chapter 23: Wealth and Power 157
Chapter 24: The Hole 164
Chapter 25: Extraction 172
Chapter 26: Negotiations 176

Chapter 27: Colton Wrancor 183
Chapter 28: Adrienne Sends a Message.................................. 190
Chapter 29: Amanda's Plan 198
Chapter 30: Recovery... 204
Chapter 31: Apologies bv Accepted 212
Chapter 32: The Send-Off 219

About the Author 223
Other books by Jeff Hill... 225

Prologue

The elderly doctor was startled by a text alert at 3:00 AM. He fumbled for his glasses on the nightstand. It took a few more seconds before he could see well enough to push the message icon on his phone. He read the text:

lat: -38.188332 long: 144.410824

He stared at the screen an extra-long moment. A hollow ache rumbled through the pit of his stomach. He knew someday this might happen. Yet he'd always hoped this was a message he would never see.

His hands quivered. It took a great effort to steady them enough to turn on the lamp.

He walked across the room to his desk and opened his laptop. He opened a map program and typed in the coordinates. A small red pin popped up. Back on his phone, he touched the top name on his list of favorites.

"My gosh, Arthur, it's three in the morning," the man on the other end said. "This better be important."

"She's in trouble."

"Are you sure?"

"The emergency S.O.S. just came in."

"Where did it come from?"

"Melbourne."

"Florida?"

"No. Australia."

"You have to find her Arthur!" the voice on the other end pleaded.

"I will."

Chapter 1
Trips to the Zoo

The first time it happened she'd just turned five.

It happened at a zoo, sort of.

* * *

"Are we there yet?" Kita asked for the third time.

"Only ten more minutes," her mom answered.

Kita loved animals. Making her first trip to a real zoo pushed her anticipation meter full-throttle. The day her mom told her they were going, she started looking at pictures on the zoo's website of all the animals she was going to see. That raised her excitement even further. However, the drive to the zoo was unbearable because her brother Zach, who was two years older, was reading a book, but wouldn't read to her. He was upset because he lost a coin toss that allowed Kita to pick the exhibit they would visit first.

"I'll read it to you if we get to see the polar bears first," he said.

"I don't care about your stupid book anyway," she said

The only noise from the back seat for the last ten minutes of the drive was Zach making a big show when he turned to the next page. Kita ignored him. At least she tried to.

When Kita jumped out of the car, she pulled on her mom's finger, dragging her faster to the front gate. She hopped in place as her mom paid for tickets and grabbed a map.

"Where is he?" Kita asked.

"This way." Her mom pointed to a path that meandered under a towering canopy of basswood trees.

She ran when she saw the massive gorilla.

"Look! Look!" she called out.

He was displayed in a round "house" made of tempered glass smudged up by a multitude of tiny fingers; all grimy from cotton candy and buttered popcorn. The enclosure was two stories tall and far enough across to park a school bus. There was a manmade tree in the middle and a moving stream of water slid along the wall on the outer edge. Thick rope ladders were suspended from the ceiling and a hammock hung below the largest branch of the fake tree. A walkway surrounded the glass on both levels. At the front of the exhibit, a pewter plaque with raised letters simply read, "Elliot."

"What does the sign say?" she asked.

"It says Elliot," Zach answered. "You should learn how to read. I could read when I was five."

"I can read," she shot back.

"Really? What does that sign say?" He pointed to a restroom sign.

"It says you're a turd."

Zach punched her in the arm.

"Ouch!" she called out.

She kicked him twice in the shin before their mom stepped between them. Kita never cried to Mommy when Zach hit her. She just hit him back, harder if she could. Even at a young age, she never tattled. She got even.

That's enough you two." She held them apart at arm's length.

Twelve little faces from a nearby daycare pressed against the glass. The great silverback had nowhere to escape. He turned his back to the crowd and pressed his face close to the gray, concrete bark.

Kita tugged on her mom's shirt and pointed through the glass.

"He has silver hair on his back just like in the pictures."

"He sure does," her mom answered.

"Why don't they have other gorillas for him to play with?" asked Zach.

"I'm not sure," she replied.

The trio stood next to the glass, staring at Elliot for a few more minutes. The giant ape did not change his posture.

"I think he's sad Mommy," Kita said.

"Why do you think that?"

"He's hanging his head and he won't look at me."

"Animals can't be sad," Zach said as if he was an authority on the subject. "They're just animals."

"Animals can be sad," Kita protested.

"How do you know?"

"Barney cries if I don't bring him with me when I go outside."

Barney was the Tenzio family dog. He was part shepherd and part collie, a huge dog with a bark that scared most people until they realized he was saying hi.

"That's just your imagination," Zach continued.

"No, it's not."

"I think it's time to go see the polar bears," suggested their mom, still standing between them.

It was their next stop.

After the polar bears, they trekked around the zoo until lunchtime. They watched the big cats stretching, threw popcorn at the seals, and slipped inside a giant net where butterflies landed on their outstretched hands. They spent the biggest block of time watching the giraffes eat from the hand of a zoo worker. He was standing high on a ladder holding out leaf-filled branches.

On the drive home, however, all Kita could talk about was *sad* Elliot.

When Kita woke up from a late afternoon nap, she made her way to the back patio. Her mom was sitting in a wicker chair reading some documents from work. Stacy Tenzio placed the papers in a briefcase and let Kita crawl onto her lap. The pair looked nothing like mother and daughter. Stacy was blonde, blue-eyed, rosy-cheeked, and tall. She looked like she just stepped off a ski slope in Norway. Kita on the other hand was short for her age. Her black hair was so thick, her mom had to keep it short to make brushing even possible. Her brown eyes looked too big for her face and her complexion was a permanent tan.

"I went and saw sad Elliot again," Kita announced.

"What are you talking about Honey?"

"I flied there. I went right into the big tree room and walked up to him. I saw his face. His eyes are sad, Mommy. He doesn't like it when people stare at him all day. His real name isn't Elliot either. It's Mahshando. It means *champion*."

"How do you know his *real* name?"

"He told me."

"I see." A wry little smirk creased Stacy's face.

"What does champion mean Mommy?"

"A champion is like a fighter or a warrior who wins the battle, or a team that wins the big game."

"I was right about him being sad."

"You were?" Stacy said playing along.

"Yes, before I flied back home he said I could come back and visit him again because then he's not so sad."

"What do you mean you *flied* there?"

"You know, I wanted to go see him real bad, so I flied through the sky all the way to the zoo. I went super-fast."

Stacy smiled and let out a slight chuckle.

"What's wrong Mommy?"

"Nothing is wrong Honey. Sounds like you had quite a dream."

"It didn't feel like a dream."

"It has to be a dream, Kita. People can't fly."

"I know that. My arms and legs and stuff didn't fly. It was the me that's inside me that flied."

"Flew," Stacy said, finally correcting her. "What do you mean when you say the me that's inside me?"

"I'm always inside my body when I dream. But when I flied…I mean flew, my inside me went out."

"Kita, you know people and animals can't talk to each other in real life, but in dreams, I suppose they can."

"We didn't talk out loud," Kita explained.

"You didn't?"

"No, we thinked at each other."

Stacy pulled Kita in a little tighter and a few seconds passed before she spoke. "This must be one of the most special dreams of all time. I think it's because of how you felt about Elliot being sad at the zoo today. We all have special dreams sometimes."

"Do you have special dreams?" she asked.

"I do, but maybe not as special as yours was today."

"Okay Mommy," Kita said snuggling closer.

* * *

Late in the evening after Zach and Kita were in bed, Stacy and Michael Tenzio cuddled on the sofa in the fireplace room.

"Something very strange happened today with Kita."

"Did she and Zach hug and hold hands?"

Stacy laughed. "I didn't say a miracle. I said strange. Our daughter's imagination blew me away today. She told me she *flew* to the zoo and talked with a silverback gorilla during her nap time."

"That's not so strange," Mike said. "She's always making up stories about animals and magic and stuff. So, her dreaming on it seems natural."

"This was different."

"How so?"

"She described an out of body experience in detail that is beyond what some five-year-old could make up or even think of. Plus, she said the gorilla told her his real name and what it meant."

"So?"

"She said his name was Mahshando and it means champion."

"I've always said this girl is going to be a writer," Mike said.

"There is one more piece."

"What?"

"I tried looking up the word online but I couldn't find anything that made sense. So, I called my friend Josie at the U. You met her at Harrison's party last fall. She teaches linguistics. You remember her?"

"Barely. She's the one with the tattoo on her ear?"

"Yes."

"And?"

"She said there is an old Bantu language from the mountain region of central Africa where the word Mahshando means *the champion.*"

"Okay, now that is too weird," Mike said.

"It's more than weird. But there is one more thing. When I asked her how she and this gorilla were able to talk to each other she said they didn't really talk, they "thinked" at each other."

"Thinked at each other?"

"Thinked at each other."

Chapter 2
Cardiac Arrest

The second time it happened was a few days before her thirteenth birthday.

Kita and her parents were watching Zach's first baseball game of the spring. Volunteer dads were the umpires. This week, Tyler Olson's dad was taking his turn behind the plate. He tried fitting into the umpire's chest protector three times before he gave up and settled for the facemask only. He was too big. There was so much flesh on his arms that his palms faced backward when he walked. His neck was like a sagging donut that stuck out farther than his chin and his stomach spilled out over his belt making it disappear.

Billy Denton hit a ball to third. Mr. Olson started waddling down the first baseline to get a better view.

He didn't make it.

He collapsed, landing on his side. He clutched his chest, with groans that sounded more like growls. Stacy was reaching for her phone before he hit the ground.

"We have an emergency at the Randall fields. Adult male… collapsed… please hurry!"

The ambulance was there in minutes. It drove over the curb and onto the field. Two paramedics rolled Mr. Olson onto the stretcher, and they recruited two dads to help lift him onto the gurney.

When the ambulance drove off, everyone stood around the backstop. A few people looked at each other. Most stared at the ground.

"I guess we'll have to replay this game later in the schedule," announced one of the coaches.

A few of the boys complained, a couple of the dads mumbled their disappointment, eventually all agreed, and everyone trudged off to the parking lot.

"I knew Tyler's dad shouldn't ump," Zach said tossing his glove and bat into the back of the Suburban.

"Keep those thoughts to yourself young man," his dad ordered.

"Yes sir."

Mike Tenzio owned a construction company with over twenty employees. He knew how to give orders. He never barked them out. He simply made calm, firm statements. Few ever argued, including Zach.

Mike walked over and put his hand on Zach's shoulder. "I know you're disappointed but you have to realize this is an unusual situation. Think about Tyler. Do you think he would want you guys to keep playing as if nothing happened?"

"I suppose not."

"All right then. Let's go home," Mike said.

Once they were on their way, Kita asked a question. "What exactly causes a heart attack?"

"There are different kinds," her dad answered, "most happen when the heart can't get enough blood to work right."

"Why can't it get enough blood?"

"Usually happens when an artery is plugged up."

"Is Mr. Olson going to die?"

"I hope not," said Stacy. "They did have him breathing pretty well with the oxygen when they drove off. Plus, there's a lot of new technology that really helps."

* * *

That evening when Stacy called Kita to come down for dinner there was no answer. She called again. Still no answer.

"Kita. I've called you twice now. We're ready to eat."

Nothing.

She went to investigate. Kita was lying motionless on her bedroom floor, not curled up like napping, but crumpled as if she had fallen out of her chair. Stacy leaned in close to Kita's face to check her breathing. It was even. She placed a finger on the side of Kita's neck. Her pulse was steady. She held her hand to Kita's forehead; no fever. She shook her.

"Wake up, Kita. Dinner is ready."

Kita didn't wake up.

Stacy ran into the hall. "Mike, come up here quick!"

"What's up?" he asked from the bottom of the stairs.

"Something is wrong with Kita. She won't wake up."

He sprinted up the stairs two at a time. He knelt beside her and placed his hand under her head.

"Wake up Kita, it's time for dinner."

She didn't wake.

He picked her up and carried her to the rocking chair. He sat down, kept her in his lap, and rested her head against his chest. He gently shook her. Still, she lay completely limp.

"Something is seriously wrong here," he said. "Call 911."

Stacy hurried across the hall to get her phone.

Kita opened her eyes.

"Wait!" Mike called, "She's awake."

"Hi, Dad," said Kita. "Why are you in my room? And how did I get on your lap?"

"We came to get you for dinner but you wouldn't wake up."

"Why did you decide to sleep on the floor?" asked Stacy when she came back into the room.

"I was sleeping?"

"Either that or you were passed out."

"I was sitting in the chair and I was worried about Mr. Olson. And then I . . ."

She hesitated and looked at her dad, unsure about saying any more.

"It's okay, sweetheart. You can tell us," Mike said.

"I'm not sure if I can."

"What do you mean?"

"I must have been dreaming, but it didn't seem like a dream."

"Tell us anyway," he said.

"Okay. As I said, I was thinking about Mr. Olson. The next thing I knew, it was like I was in his hospital room standing right next to his bed, but no one could see me. I kept saying hi, but no one could hear me. I thought maybe I was dreaming but then…"

"Then what?"

"The doctor came in and talked with Mrs. Olson. He said words I didn't know."

"What kind of words?"

"Angioplastic something, and stent, and cardiac arrest."

Mike smiled. "It's angioplasty."

"Can I have words in my dreams I don't even know?" Kita asked.

Mike pulled her close.

"I'm not sure. That's a big question for a little girl."

"I'm not a little girl anymore," Kita reminded her father. "In two days I'm a teenager."

"Excuse me," her dad said, smiling. "Still, it must have been a powerfully strong dream because we couldn't wake you for anything.

As far as the words you're not familiar with, you know your mom and I were discussing all these things on the way home from the baseball game. That's probably when you heard them."

"I heard Mrs. Olson tell the doctor it was okay to operate. She had to sign papers. What about that?" Kita continued.

"Like I said," Mike answered, "powerful dream."

"One more thing," she said. "When I decided to come back, I was back."

"Think about it Honey," Mike explained, "in our dreams, we can fly, travel through time, be other people, be places we've never been, fall off a cliff and wake up before we hit. It's unlimited what can happen in dreams."

"Maybe you're right," Kita said.

"Well, let's go eat. We'll talk about big huge dreams later."

"Mom?"

"Yes, Kita."

Do you ever *travel* in your dreams? You know, like supernatural travel?" Kita studied her face looking for the truth.

"I think so, but I've never remembered it as well as you."

* * *

After dinner, Stacy went into her bedroom, closed the door, and picked up her phone. Brenda Olson's number was in her favorites.

"Brenda? It's Stacy. Just wanted to check in and see how Derek was doing."

"He's in surgery right now," Brenda answered. "They are going to try angioplasty in two places and also give him a stent."

An uncomfortable fluttering began twisting in Stacy's stomach.

"They think he'll be okay. They don't think he suffered any major cardiac muscle damage. We're lucky. Maybe this will be a big enough scare that he'll get serious now about losing weight."

"I am glad to hear that. Is Tyler with you?"

"Yes."

"I'll come by and pick him up. He can stay with us tonight."

"That's not necessary."

"Come on, Brenda."

"Okay. Thank you, Stacy."

Stacy's hand trembled when she pushed the red phone icon to disconnect. She knew she and Mike talked about cardiac muscles in the car, but they never once used angioplasty or stent in their conversation. She tried to stir a faint and distant memory of a dream and a trip to the zoo years earlier, but couldn't quite reach it.

Chapter 3
The Champion

Kita was unable to will herself to sleep that night. Counting backward didn't work, either did reciting all the words she could think of that started with *K*. Her mind was swirling around events at the hospital. She was sure enough of herself to know what was a dream and what wasn't. What she couldn't figure out was, if she didn't have a dream, what did she have? And how did it happen? Then she remembered another special dream from years before about a zoo and a big gorilla. She even remembered his name. She remembered her promise.

And then, she was out.

She hovered over her body which was still lying under the blanket and was amazed she was no longer inside. She could hardly believe her eyes when she drifted through her window. She went in and out of her room two more times to be sure.

This is crazy.

Then she floated higher. She was hesitant to go above the trees. When she realized she wasn't going to fall, she shot up a hundred feet or so. She was terrified and thrilled at the same time. The lights of the city looked like thousands of pinholes poking out of black velvet cloth. She didn't know how to find the zoo and couldn't remember how she did it the first time. She started scanning, and without deliberately trying, her eyes started to zoom in on places. They kept zooming and she kept scanning until she recognized the lights of the zoo.

In a moment she was standing outside the glass walls of the gorilla house.

The pewter sign still read Elliot. He was laying down on his hammock, spread out between two branches. He sat up when he saw her. The thick fur on his arms made them look puffy. A patch of brown covered his forehead and Kita could see moisture droplets on the outer edge of his nostrils.

"Can you see me?" Kita asked.

"Yes."

"Do you remember me? I visited once when I was smaller."

"I remember," said Mahshando, "but you never came back."

"I know. I'm sorry. I didn't know I could come back. I thought it was just a dream. I was only five, you know."

"What's five?"

"You know, *years*."

"I don't know years."

"How do you tell time then?" Kita asked.

"Moons."

"Oh. Well, I think there are twelve or thirteen new moons in a year," Kita said.

"I see. And how many years are you now?"

"Almost thirteen."

"You're still small."

"I can't help it if I'm short."

"I suppose that's true."

"Anyway, today I went to a hospital and I knew it wasn't a dream. Then I remembered when I came to you. So I tried again and I got here."

"You can come in if you'd like." Mahshando held out an open hand.

She slipped through the glass as if it wasn't there, still amazed she could pass through solid glass without feeling anything. The pungent smell of gorilla was overwhelming. She refused to plug her nose. She thought it would be rude.

"I don't know your name?" he said.

"Kita."

"Why have you come this night?"

"Tonight I finally remembered you said I could come to visit and then you wouldn't be so sad."

"So I did."

"Have you always lived here?" she asked.

"When I was a baby I lived in the trees and the tall grass with my family. One day, I fell into a deep pit and a giant net dropped on me. Men trapped me in the net and took me away from my home. I traveled across huge water where you couldn't see any land. Then they put me in a noisy box and brought me here."

"How long have you been here?"

"More moons than I can count."

"You should escape."

"The only way out is there." Mahshando pointed to a narrow door hidden behind a fake boulder.

Kita examined the door. She tried jiggling the handle but her hand just passed through it. She tried pushing on the door. Her arm went through that as well. She reached for one of the ropes above her head. It was like grabbing at thin air. Kita could smell Mahshando's musky scent. She could hear the stream moving along the glass wall, and taste the air, but she could not feel anything she tried to touch.

Mahshando watched.

"It looks like you can't hang on to anything," he said.

Kita passed through the door to see the other side. There was a large bolt that slid into a bracket on the frame. She came back into the cage.

"Are you strong?" she asked.

"I am strong." He beat his chest with two resounding thuds.

"Come here then," Kita instructed.

Mahshando swung down from his perch on the hammock.

"Kick with your feet as hard as you can right here." Kita pointed to a spot right next to the handle.

Mahshando lay on his back and kicked at the door. It didn't budge. He kicked again. No effect. Then he pushed the boulder aside and cleared a path from one end of the cage to the door. He stepped back as far as he could and ran. Six feet from his target he leaped feet first and crashed into the door. It rattled and loosened. On the third try, the door burst open and Mahshando squeezed his massive body through the opening.

There was a loud ruckus from the other animals as Kita and Mahshando strolled through the zoo. The chimps were hopping up and down and screeching. A male lion let out a roar so loud Kita could feel the vibration and the elephants responded with trumpet calls of their own. All the entrances to the enclosures were secured with the same kind of sliding bolt that held Mahshando's door. Kita explained to him how to slide the bolt and open the doors. Soon, tigers and wolves and zebras and lions and even giraffes were strolling about the zoo.

The lemurs scurried to the top branches of the cottonwood trees and screeched, "Free! Free! Free!" as loud as they could.

The bears went straight to the snack bar that was directly in front of their enclosure. One of them bashed in the side door. Then they stuffed themselves with chocolate bars, leftover cotton candy, Cracker Jacks, and giant slabs of taffy. Two warthogs kept banging at a dumpster but they couldn't tip it over. Mahshando grabbed the side and tipped it over for them. They rutted through the garbage munching on half-eaten hot dogs, moldy sandwiches, and stale popcorn.

"They'll eat anything," Mahshando explained to Kita.

Only the ornery orangutan had a negative word. "Where are we supposed to get our fruit if we leave?"

Mahashando stood face to face with him and poked him in the chest. "Stay if you like."

In short order the big cats and the wolves were off and running, leaving the prison of the zoo far behind. Before they left, each stopped and bowed to Kita and to Mahshando and gave thanks. Kita greeted every single one.

A giraffe named, 'Lingle' lowered her head to Kita's ear. "You are a princess," she said.

When most of the departure ceremonies were over, an ancient elephant ambled over to Kita and Mahshando. She stared at Kita.

"Are you Adrienne?" She dropped her head to get a better look.

"No. I'm Kita. What's your name?"

"I am Mtotah." She rose back up to her full height.

"Who's Adrienne?" Kita asked.

"A young human girl I knew long ago. You look like her."

"If you knew her long ago, wouldn't she be old now?"

"Yes. But she was like you."

"What do you mean?"

"I could talk to her also when she was traveling."

"Traveling?" Kita's body tensed.

"Outside her other body," Mtotah explained.

Kita shivered. The elephant's words frightened her. She felt isolated and exposed.

"I think I better go back," she said to Mahshando.

He reached out to pat her head.

"Can you feel me?" she asked.

"Yes."

"I wonder why I can't feel you?"

Mtotah rubbed her trunk on Kita's side. Kita could not feel that either.

"I hope they don't catch you," Kita said, before leaving.

In an instant, she was back in her room, in her body, and under the covers. She felt tired and her muscles had an ever so slight twinge of pain, but she didn't think anything of it.

What is happening to me? There is somebody else that can do this that looks like me? Why am I scared? What if someone finds out?

All her questions added to her exhaustion and she drifted off to sleep.

* * *

The Eureka Tower dominated Melbourne's skyline. Only one resident occupied the eighty-seventh floor. Behind his back, his employees called him Bayne, or worse, but in his presence, they addressed him as sir. Everyday people he interacted with knew him as Mr. Bayne, while victims and enemies preferred to never speak his name. Tonight's visitor to the top of the world was not offered a chair. No one ever was.

"Why are you here?" Bayne demanded.

"I'm sorry to disturb you, sir, but I was quite sure you would want to hear this personally."

Claude Bayne leaned back in his black leather chair. The lamps in the room were fixed in such a way that his face remained in shadow.

Sitting at attention by his side, as always, was Cerberus, an oversized Rhodesian Ridgeback. The muscles of his neck and shoulders rippled under his hide. His eyes followed the visitor's every move. A low, rumbling growl, hung deep in his throat.

Bayne took a long pull on his cigar, sipped his bourbon, and motioned for the man to continue.

"Your 'special guest' had a break from her routine."

"How so?"

"Every day is the same. She eats, she exercises, she never says a word, and she goes into that trance thing."

"Go on."

"Today when she was doing her trance, she started smiling and she whispered something."

"What did she say?"

"We've double-checked the audio, but we're pretty sure it was, 'she knows.'"

Bayne's expression remained unchanged, but he rose out of his chair, stepped behind it, and paced. He fingered a solid gold cigar lighter is his pants pocket, an old habit he'd acquired whenever he was contemplating his next move.

"You were right to tell me," he finally said. "Any progress with the phone?"

"It died. The tech guy says the chip is fried like it self-destructed when he tried to unlock her password. That's the other reason I came personally. I knew you wanted this." The visitor handed the phone to Bayne.

"How about escape attempts?"

"The first two days she went to the edge of the shock zone in every direction possible and tried to get the anklet off. It appears that she's given up."

"That will be all then." Bayne waved him away. A panel on the teak covered wall opened and the man stepped into the elevator.

Cerberus gave him a parting growl.

"Good boy."

Bayne scratched Cerberus behind the ears and dimmed the lights two more notches. Then he ran his index finger along an old scar that stretched from ear to shoulder on the left side of his neck. He took a long swallow of his drink. He wondered who the 'she' was, and he wondered what kind of person carries a self-destructing phone. *It is time I pay our special guest a visit*, he thought to himself.

Chapter 4
Elliot Makes the News

The lead story on every local television station the next morning focused on vandals breaking into Park City's Capitol Zoo and releasing the animals. The giraffes and elephants had been rounded up, but as of yet, there was no sign of the big cats, the wolves, or the gorilla.

"Can you believe that?" asked Zach in between bites of scrambled eggs.

Kita watched as a young reporter from Channel 5 interviewed an elderly woman who was in total shock after waking up and finding two giraffes nibbling away at a box elder tree in her backyard.

Then the news story switched to the zoo. Connie Smythe, the head administrator of Capitol Zoo was on camera first.

"I am so disappointed something like this could happen," she said.

Stuart Regent, Park City's Chief of Police was next.

"I am committed to finding those responsible," he declared.

Kita didn't like the idea of being found responsible.

Barney came to her like he did every morning, tongue hanging out, and tail wagging. Most mornings, a good portion of Kita's breakfast often found its way to the kitchen floor. Barney never missed a scrap.

Kita had an idea. She stared at Barney and tried to think a thought to him.

If you can hear me put your paw on my leg, she thought with all her might.

Nothing.

She concentrated harder.

Still nothing.

She finished her eggs and let a half a slice of bacon slip to the floor.

Barney wolfed it down without taking a chew.

Then Kita remembered what Mtotah said about talking with Adrienne when she was *traveling*. She ran up to her room and laid on the floor. Then she left her body and went back down to the kitchen. Barney barked when he saw her.

"What are you barking at?" asked Zach.

Barney turned toward Zach and barked louder.

"It's okay Barney. It's really me," said Kita.

Barney stopped barking.

"You don't look the same. I can't smell you either, and now you can talk to me?"

"I don't know how it works," answered Kita, "somehow I can leave my body and talk to animals."

"Where's the rest of you?"

"In my room."

"What are you looking at, you crazy dog?" asked Zach.

"He's looking at me," Kita said. "Can't you see me?"

Zach went over and scratched the top of Barney's head.

"What are you looking at boy?" he asked again.

Kita waved her hand in front of Zach's face. He saw nothing. She tried tapping him on the shoulder, no reaction.

"Can't he see you?" asked Barney.

"I guess not. Let's go to my room."

Barney sprinted up the stairs. She beat him there.

"See, that's the real me there on the floor and this other me is here too."

Barney sniffed the Kita lying on the floor and licked her hand.

"How come you haven't done this before?" Barney asked.

"Until yesterday, I didn't know I could. Can you understand me when I talk to you in my regular body?" Kita asked.

"Only a few things, mostly I read your face and your sounds."

"I'm going back into my body now," Kita said. "I have to go to school. I'll come back later."

Once back in her body she sat up and petted him under his chin. He groaned with pleasure.

* * *

Behind closed doors, the scene between Connie Smythe and Stuart Regent was quite different than their performance for the television cameras.

"Let me see that again," Stuart Regent said.

He, along with Connie Smythe, were watching a video feed recorded the night before. The entire zoo grounds were under twenty-four-hour video surveillance and all of Elliot's actions were recorded. They kept re-watching his running smashes into the door of the gorilla house.

"He keeps turning his head off to the side as if he's looking at something," Regent said.

"But there's nothing there," Smythe answered.

"Why, after all these years would this happen? And how could he figure out running at the door, or even lying on his back and kicking?" Regent asked.

"I don't know but it gets stranger than this."

The next clip showed Elliot going around to different doors and sliding open the bolts.

"That is not possible," Regent declared. He started pacing. "This video never leaves this room. There is no way we are going to let the public know there's a giant silverback running around town who knows how to open bolted doors! Agreed?"

"Agreed," Smythe answered.

"Look at what the animals do before they leave the zoo," Smythe continued.

"It looks like they are bowing or something, even the lions," Regent said.

"I know. It's incredible."

They watched one final piece of video. The oldest elephant of the zoo and the great silverback were standing side by side looking at a blank space in front of them. Then the gorilla reached out his hand like he was patting something and the elephant rubbed her trunk up and down like she was stroking an imaginary tree.

"What do you make of that?" asked Chief Regent.

"I've never seen anything like it," Smythe answered.

* * *

In a well-fashioned log home on a remote and isolated island in the frigid waters of Lake Superior, Dr. Arthur Armitauge was watching the local news coming out of Duluth. The strange events of Park City's zoo dominated the broadcast. It had his full attention. When it was over he went to his computer and watched it again.

"Where's the video feed?" he wondered to himself.

Then he read every internet story he could find on Park City's Capitol Zoo. They all reported the same thing. The video surveillance system had been hacked and disabled before the breakouts occurred. "Highly organized animal activists," was the official statement of Park City's chief of police.

He grabbed his phone. Francis was the name atop his list of favorites.

"Have you seen the news from the zoo at Park City?" the good doctor asked.

"No."

"Go online and watch it. Then see if Gabriel can get into the zoo's computer system. I want to be positive there is no video."

"Anything else?"

"Nothing yet. If we get a video, we'll decide then."

Chapter 5
Amanda Griffith

There were three houses in the loop of Kita's cul-de-sac. The Tenzios were in the middle. To the east were the Brantley's. They didn't like Barney much, which meant Kita didn't like them much either.

"Something was terribly wrong with people who don't like animals," she told her mom.

To the west were the Griffiths. They had four kids, Amanda, the youngest, was the only one still at home. She was a year older than Kita but they were in the same grade at school. Amanda had to do second grade twice because she had been sick with some bizarre cancer and was in the hospital for almost a whole year. They had been best friends since forever. She was at the bus stop when Kita walked out. Today her hair was bright copper.

"Hey, I like the new color," said Kita.

"Thanks. I was getting tired of blue."

Amanda dyed her hair a new color every month or so. She also wore vests. They came in more colors than a bag of Skittles. Today was orange. She always and only wore black pants, but she alternated between red, purple, green, and yellow high top canvas shoes. Her oversized black-framed glasses looked out of place on her slender face.

"Did you hear about the zoo?" Amanda asked.

"Yeah," answered Kita, still trying to reassure herself no one would *find her responsible.*

"I think it's fabulous," Amanda continued.

"Who do you think did it?" Kita asked.

"I think it's that group from California. They're doing all kinds of stuff like that. You know they put a stop to that testing lab in San Francisco last year."

"You're probably right," agreed Kita.

The bus driver smiled when she opened the doors for the girls.

"Hey look. Squat has a new pet. It's a copperhead."

This verbal assault was called out by Ben Longstreet. He hated Kita. She felt the same. It started in third grade when he teased her about being short and bug-eyed. Later that same day on the playground, she squirted a bottle of water all over the front of his pants, pointed at him, and yelled, "Look, everybody. Ben peed his pants!" They'd been enemies ever since. He called her Squat, and Kita called him Longstream.

"For your information, Ben Longstream," Amanda broke in. "Copperhead snakes bite humans more than any other snake in North America. They're poisonous and they eat their prey whole. Of course, you wouldn't know that because you actually have to know how to read to get that information."

"Every time you open your mouth you prove you're a freakoid," Ben sneered back.

"Yeah, we can read just fine," said Harold Wartworth. "We just don't read stupid science books all day."

"You know what, Warthog, I saw you guys reading a nature book the other day," Kita said.

"Oh yeah, what was that?"

"Curious George Goes to the Zoo."

Most of the kids laughed until Ben Longstreet stood up and stared them down.

Harold Wartworth was always at Ben Longstreet's side; followed him around like a puppy. Of course, the poor kid had a horrible last name and his parents were clueless enough to name him Harold. Harry Warthog is a hard nickname to live with. Kita would have felt sorry for him if he wasn't friends with Ben Longstreet.

The girls sat as far away from the hated duo as they could.

"I got you something really cool for your birthday," Amanda gushed.

"Tell me," said Kita.

"No. You have to wait until tomorrow."

Lunch and first-hour science were the only time the girl's schedules meshed. Amanda was in all the advanced classes, but the school had no advanced science. She played the cello in the orchestra and the piano for the honors choir. Kita slogged through with the *average* kids and the only musical instrument she played was iTunes.

"I might be book smart, but you're street smart," Amanda encouraged her one time.

"I wish they had street smart on my report card," Kita countered.

Today in science they had a test. When Amanda placed her completed test on Mr. Granlund's desk, Kita was still stuck on the first page.

* * *

"Look at this," Amanda told Kita when they sat down at lunch. She handed Kita her phone. A breaking news story reported that all the monkeys and lemurs from the zoo had been recaptured. The only animals yet to be caught were four of the big cats, two of the wolves, and the silverback gorilla.

"At least they were free for a while," Kita said. Inside she was hoping against hope that Mahshando would never be found.

* * *

It was a crisp and sunny day so the girls decided to walk.

"Stop over for a minute, will you?" asked Amanda when they reached the cul-de-sac. "I thought I could wait 'til tomorrow to show you your present, but I can't."

"Okay."

"She's in the back shed," Amanda said.

"She?" Kita asked.

"Yeah, your gift is a . . ."

They both froze. Standing between them and the shed was a Bengal tiger. He studied them with a level gaze. His nostrils opened wide and drops of moisture dripped off the tip of his tongue.

"What do we do?" whispered Amanda.

"Don't move," Kita commanded.

"I don't think I could if I wanted to."

Amanda was shaking and her face looked like it belonged on a poster advertising a horror movie.

Gradually, with deliberate steps, the tiger moved toward them. The closer he got, the slower he went. His giant footpads were soundless on the grass. He stopped in front of Kita and stared. He was so big, and Kita so short, he hardly had to look up. His face was so close to Kita's she could see the tiny fibers on his whiskers and smell his breath.

"He's staring at you!" Amanda whispered.

"I know."

"This is really scaring me." Amanda reached for Kita's arm.

Kita could feel Amanda's tremors.

"I need you to do something for me," Kita said.

"What?"

"Hold me by the arm and don't let me fall."

"Fall?"

"You have to hold on. Trust me."

Kita leaned her weight into Amanda and her body went limp. Amanda wrapped her arms around Kita.

A look of surprise swept over Amanda, but she held on, letting Kita rest against her side.

Kita was out.

The tiger turned away from the physical Kita and focused on the Kita who was invisible to Amanda.

"Are you are the girl who freed us? he asked.

"Yes, my name is Kita."

"I thought that girl might be you," he motioned his head to Kita's body resting against Amanda's side. "You look the same, but different."

"I am both."

"How can that be?"

"I'm not sure. I just know it is."

"One person is two?"

"I haven't figured it out yet but I'm trying," Kita said. "What's your name anyway?"

"I am Saamradi."

"Why are you here?" Kita asked.

"I am following the path of the sun. I am hungry and I smelled food in there." He nodded to a garage size shed built along the back property line.

"Wait here," Kita instructed. At the speed of thought, she was in the shed. A cute, fluffy, golden retriever puppy was in a kennel. At the same speed, she was back standing in front of Saamradi.

"You can't eat the puppy. I will get you food, but you have to be quiet. And the other girl is my friend, you can't hurt her either. Promise?"

"I promise."

Kita's slumping body came back to life.

"What happened to you?" Amanda asked.

"We have to go to my house, quick."

"What about the …?"

Saamradi followed them.

"He's following us." Amanda kept looking backward, staring in disbelief.

"He won't hurt us."

"How in the world do you know that? We need to run."

"You can't outrun a tiger. Just come with me and stay calm."

"Calm? Sure. No problem. Tigers follow me every day."

Kita skipped down the basement stairs and pulled two chickens out of the freezer. She ripped off the wrapping and threw them into the microwave, cranked it on high, and waited five minutes. Saamradi sat down a few yards from the back door. Amanda looked totally stupefied and Barney was whimpering.

"Will you explain what in the world is going on around here?" Amanda asked.

"He is hungry and he promised not to eat you or the puppy if I got him something to eat."

"What?! He promised not to eat me?! What do you mean *he promised*? How do you know about the puppy?"

"I'll explain everything later."

The microwave dinged and Kita took out the chickens. They weren't completely thawed, but they were good enough. She carried them out the back door. Saamradi stood while Kita placed the chickens at his feet. Monstrous crunching sounds echoed off the back wall of the house as he wolfed down the partially frozen chickens, bones and all.

Kita petted him on the top of his head before she sat down on the back step.

"Hold me one more time, Amanda, so I don't fall over."

"You are freaking me out."

"Please."

Amanda sat next to Kita. She never took her eyes off the tiger. Kita went out again and Amanda held her limp body.

"I'm sorry I don't have more food for you," Kita said.

"This food helped," Saamradi answered.

"Where will you go now?"

"I will follow the sun until I am at home."

Kita didn't have the heart to tell him that home was across the Pacific Ocean.

"What if they catch you?"

"They won't catch me alive. I am not going back to the cage."

"What about Mahshando?"

"I have not seen him since I escaped."

With that, Saamradi made his way to a dirt path leading out the back of the property and headed west.

"Be careful," Kita called out.

He turned and bowed low to the ground before he disappeared down the lane.

When Kita returned to her body, she stood up and faced Amanda who was shaking and muttering to herself.

"There is something I have to tell you," Kita said.

"No duh," said Amanda. "I swear that tiger just bowed, and what's with the passing out thing?"

"First, you have to promise me you will tell absolutely no one. And second, you have to promise not to laugh. And third, you have to promise not to think I'm crazy."

"Just tell me already," demanded Amanda.

"I haven't told anyone what I am about to tell you, and even though you are the truest friend a person could have, I'm still afraid to tell you."

The seriousness of Kita's words caused Amanda to straighten up a bit.

"You can tell me. I won't tell a soul," she promised.

"Well… I… ah… this week I discovered I have some unusual abilities."

"What kind of abilities?"

"This is going to sound weird."

"Tell me already."

Kita was afraid Amanda wouldn't believe her. Worse yet, she didn't know what to do if she didn't.

"I can travel outside my body, and when I do, I can communicate with animals." Hearing herself saying it out loud, made it sound crazy, even to her.

Amanda laughed. "Very funny."

"I knew you wouldn't believe me." Kita lowered her head and turned away.

"You can't expect me to believe you have some kind of superpowers? That's whacko, Kita."

"You promised you wouldn't think I was crazy."

"No, you said I had to promise. I just promised I wouldn't tell anyone. Don't worry about that. I'm not telling people you think you can travel outside your body. They'll think I'm as nuts as you."

"You have to believe me," pleaded Kita. "If you don't, I don't know what I'm going to do."

Kita wiped tears from her cheeks with her sleeve.

"You're crying," Amanda said. "I'm sorry. I believe you."

"You're just saying that 'cause I'm crying."

"Well —"

"The reason I had you hold me, is that when I leave my body it goes limp like I'm sleeping. I saw the puppy in the garage when I talked to the tiger. The puppy was in a little kennel. It's a golden. And you're right, the tiger did bow after I told him to be careful."

"You told him to be careful. You had a little *sit down* with him did you?"

"It's not like talking out loud. It's not exactly words either. It's like thought to thought."

"Leave your body *and* have telepathic powers with animals? Next, you're going to tell me you have X-ray vision or something."

"Let me prove it. I will go get Barney. When I'm gone, type three things you want Barney to do on the notepad on your phone. When he comes, hold out your phone so I can see it. Barney will do each trick."

"Are you serious?" asked Amanda.

"I've never been more serious about anything in my life. I'm going to lay on the ground so I don't fall over."

"If you say so."

Kita laid on the ground, left her body, and went inside to fetch Barney.

"Come outside," she told him. "I need you to do some tricks for Amanda."

"Is that great big animal I smelled earlier still out there?" Barney asked.

"It was a tiger but he's gone now."

"A tiger?"

"He's gone. Plus, I already fed him."

"Are you sure?"

"I'm sure," Kita said.

They went outside and Barney stood facing Amanda. Amanda held her phone screen up and Kita read each note.

Item 1: Run around the house one time and when you get back, sit facing away from me.

Barney took off and was back in a few seconds. He sat with his back to Amanda.

Item 2: Bark three times. Stop and bark two more.

Woof, woof, woof . . . woof, woof.

Item 3: Put your mouth around my wrist like you are going to bite me but don't clamp down.

Amanda pushed her arm forward and Barney stretched his mouth around her wrist as gentle as a baby.

"That's a good boy, Barney," Kita gushed. "I'll give you a treat."

"Just so you know, I like bacon raw better than cooked," Barney informed her.

"Kita, can you hear me?" Amanda was shaking in disbelief.

Silence.

"If you can hear me, tell Barney to lie on his back."

Two seconds later, Barney was on his back, spread-eagled with feet quivering.

"Oh my God, Kita! Oh my God!" Amanda stood up and walked in circles.

Kita returned to her body and sat up. Amanda rushed to her, jumped up and down, and hugged her.

"I believe you. This is the most incredible thing in the world! I mean I believe you, but who could believe this?"

"Tell no one," Kita reminded her.

"No one. I promise. But do you realize the implications?"

"What implications?"

"You might not be human, or maybe you're more than human, or maybe you're just a human with superpowers."

"I can't think about all that."

"Why? You have to," Amanda said.

"It's a little scary."

"It's not scary. It's exciting! It's incredible!" Amanda was walking in circles again.

"That's because it's not happening to you," Kita said.

Chapter 6
Camera Angles

Above Amanda's bed was a giant poster of Einstein, with her favorite quote: *Everyone has genius, but if you judge a fish by its ability to climb a tree you will live your whole life believing it is stupid.* The wall next to her closet was papered with the periodic table of elements, and a model of the Saturn 5 rocket was on her desk. Except for a box full of Marvel comics and a stack of graphic novels, most of her books were about science and math. Two giant bean bag chairs sat on either side of her window. The girls each sunk into their own chair, eating ice cream cones.

"You really are a nerd," Kita said. She told Amanda this every time she was in her room.

"And you wish you were," Amanda answered back as usual.

"There's something else I have to tell you about yesterday," Kita said. "I'm the one who let the animals out of their cages at the zoo."

"What?"

"Well, not me exactly. I showed Mahshando how to slide the bolts. He opened all the cages."

"Who is Mahshando?"

"That's Elliot the gorilla's real name."

"This keeps getting better," Amanda gushed.

"One other thing?"

"What?"

"An old elephant came and asked me if my name was Adrienne. She said she knew someone long ago who looked like me and was a *traveler* also, and she could talk to animals too."

"She called you a *traveler?*"

"She knew I was outside my regular body."

"That means other people can do this too," Amanda said.

"I know."

"You realize this is blowing my mind, right? It just keeps getting bigger and bigger!" Amanda got out of her chair and waved her arms in a swooping arc.

"How do you think I feel?" Kita answered.

"What else do you think you can do?"

"So far I know I can go super fast. In fact, I just show up where I want to. But I think I have to know where the place is first. I can go through walls and glass and stuff. I've got all my senses except touch. When I try to touch or grab something my hands just pass through. I have to hover, otherwise I sink into the ground. And I have zoom vision."

"Zoom vision?"

"Yeah, if I am looking at something really far away, I can zoom in and see it like it's super close. Telescopic."

"Unbelievable."

"Oh, and I am pretty sure I am invisible to humans. But I'm worried about something."

"What's that"

"You know the Chief of Police lied about the video monitoring system being hacked into."

"Of course," said Amanda, her eyes brightening with understanding. "There was no break-in, so there was no hacking. But why would they lie?"

Amanda started pacing.

"I'm not sure, but what if I'm not invisible to cameras?"

"Let's find out," suggested Amanda. "Go over in front of my door and I'll take a picture and we will see."

Kita swallowed her last bite of ice cream and slouched further into the bean bag. Then she was out hovering in front of Amanda's door. Amanda gave her a couple of seconds and then took two still photos plus a twenty-second video.

"Okay. Let's look," said Amanda.

Kita returned.

The girls studied Amanda's phone. Neither picture had any sign of Kita, but on the video, if you looked close, there was a distortion, like the way heat waves look above a fire. They replayed it a few times to be sure. It was faint and barely visible, but it was there.

"Were you moving at all?"

"I waved to you," Kita said.

"You would have to know what you're looking for to see that," Amanda said. "Even if you saw it, there's no shape, and we can see right through. No one would have any idea."

Kita watched one more time.

"You're probably right," she said. But in her heart of hearts, she was not so sure.

"What about your clothes?" Amanda asked. "Are you wearing clothes when you travel? Are you naked?"

"That's weird too. I'm not wearing my clothes but I'm not naked. I can't explain it. It's like my skin covers me in some different way. I haven't paid that close attention. I will next time."

"Let's make next time right now."

"You're pretty amped up about this," Kita said. Amanda's eyes were gleaming. Kita hadn't seen her this excited since she won the state science fair last year.

"Just once more," she said.

"Okay."

When Kita came out she examined her *traveling* body closely. Her skin was like an ultra-thin scuba suit covering her completely. It was almost scaly and it shimmered. She rotated her arm and the colors changed as she moved. It was coppery and bronze and then it wasn't. She went and stood in front of Amanda's full-length mirror. Blank

"My skin is like a tight bodysuit. But I'm not wearing it. It's part of me," she said when she returned.

"This is crazy. You have superpowers plus your own special bodysuit. This is Stan Lee stuff."

"When I move, it shimmers and changes colors. It's actually pretty cool. I don't show up in the mirror either. I checked."

They sat in silence for a few minutes trying to digest the enormity of it all.

Amanda spoke first. "If you can do thought to thought with animals what about people? Maybe you can read minds."

"I don't know. I've only been doing this for two days."

"Let's try," said Amanda. "Leave your body again and I will try to think a thought to you."

"You said just once more last time."

"This time for sure," Amanda promised.

"All right."

Kita relaxed deep into the bean bag once again and then stood next to Amanda. She could tell that Amanda was concentrating and trying to send her some thoughts. But there no were thoughts to be heard.

"Nothing," Kita said when she returned.

"Are you going to tell your parents?" asked Amanda.

"Do you think I should?"

"I wouldn't. Your parents are kind of strict you know. I mean they won't even get you a phone. Can you imagine what they'd do if they found out you can float around the universe at will?"

"Maybe you're right. Anyway, it's late, I better get going."

* * *

Kita pulled her quilt to her chin. Her mind wandered to Mtotah, the ancient elephant. She decided to pay her another visit.

Getting to the zoo was much easier this time. She didn't have to look for it. She simply thought about where she wanted to go, and she was there. Mtotah lay sleeping on a bed of loosely spread straw. Her skin was wrinkly and gray with wisps of hair scattered about her hulking frame. Her massive ears rested on the side of her head and her trunk was spread out like an uncoiled anaconda. The smell of elephant was strong, like old wet leather.

Kita stood close and whispered in her ear. "Mtotah, it's me, Kita."

Mtotah stirred and opened her eyes. She lumbered up to her feet when she saw Kita.

"Are you alright?" Kita asked.

"I am fine."

"I'm sorry about all this happening," Kita offered.

"It is okay Kita. To roam for even a day was a good thing."

"How did they find you? Did they hurt you?"

"We elephants aren't particularly good at hiding. No one tried to hurt us. You're not planning on getting us out again are you?"

"No. Besides, that was more of Mahshando's idea than it was mine. I came to talk to you if it's okay."

"What does a human girl want to talk to an old elephant about?"

"Adrienne."

"I see."

"I have only known about this *travel* ability for two days. I don't know anything. I thought maybe if there were others, I might be able to find out what's happening to me."

Mtotah eased herself down until her backside was resting on the ground. "I will tell you what I know. When I first came to a house of cages I was a baby and it was in a different place. The first night I was crying for my mother and Adrienne came. She was young like you and looked like you. She stayed with me and helped me with my loneliness that night and many others. Then one night she told me she was going to a special school and might not be able to come and see me as often."

"Did she ever come back?"

"No, and then I was moved to this place. This is not where we met. It has been 23,617 nights since I last saw her. I started counting and never stopped."

"You can count?"

"Of course I can count. All elephants can count."

Kita did some estimating. "That's over sixty years ago."

"Years?"

"One year is 365 nights," Kita explained.

"I see."

"What was her last name?" Kita asked.

"Last name?"

"You know, like first name, last name."

"I have never heard of first name, last name. Just name. You are Kita, I'm Mtotah, and Adrienne is Adrienne."

"Have you ever met any other *travelers*?"

"No. But Adrienne said at her special school, she was going to learn more about being a *traveler*. Oh, and there is one more thing."

"What's that?"

"You must be careful. Adrienne said there are watchers."

"Watchers?"

"There are some who can see you when you travel. And

remember, you can't trust all animals even if you can talk to them."

Kita's mind went into overdrive. There was so much she wanted to know:

Special school meant someone knew a great deal about what was happening to her.

There are watchers who might know about her already.

Some animals maybe aren't good (she had a hard time believing that one, except for hyenas maybe).

There is someone out there that looks just like me.

And elephants can count.

She was determined to discover it all but had no idea where to start.

When she returned to her bed she was surprised how tired she was. She also felt soreness in her arms and legs, a sensation new to her.

Must be too much excitement. She was sleeping in minutes.

Chapter 7
The Interview

Bayne decided the time had come to introduce himself to his *guest*. She had been in his possession three days but was still a mystery. Her credit card was pre-paid, untraceable. He determined her ID was real, but he was not confident it was truthful. He kept her on his estate north of Melbourne. It had been a sheep station in its day, now it was Bayne's personal compound, twenty square miles, remote, and private. She was fed well and allowed to roam the grounds. If it wasn't for the guards, the dogs, cameras everywhere, and the ankle collar, it would appear she truly was a guest.

* * *

The capture of Adrienne was a combination of extreme luck on Bayne's part and an equal amount of carelessness on Adrienne's. She had just completed a grueling two-week assignment for the U.S. State Department. The Americans were in negotiations with an uncooperative Middle Eastern country with bad intentions on how they planned to use their chemical weapons. Adrienne would secretly observe the opposition when they were meeting by themselves. She would then report to the lead negotiator for the U.S. what the Mid-East country was saying behind closed doors, and what secrets they wanted to remain secret. When the negotiations ended she decided she needed a vacation. She had always wanted to visit Uluru, the great rock that towered a thousand feet high in the middle of the flat land of the Australian outback.

Yulara is a small resort town a few miles north of the rock. It is the only place for miles that has hotels for tourists. The week that Adrienne chose to visit was also when a certain Colton Wrancor, happened to be there. He was in his late twenties. No one could figure out how light blue eyes went with his thick wavy black hair and light brown skin. He kept his six-foot frame in good condition. That, combined with his good looks, and a seemingly endless supply of money, attracted girls at any pace he desired. His companion this week was Brandy, a curvy strawberry-blonde who wasn't exactly valedictorian material.

Wrancor, Brandy, and Adrienne joined nine others in the evening van ride out to the gigantic monolith. Once there, they transferred to electric golf carts that transported them to the base of the cliffs. Adrienne's cart was two spaces ahead of Wrancor's. He didn't notice her until a small group of rock wallabies approached her cart. They are normally nocturnal creatures and extremely skittish around people. But this group came right up to her. One even climbed onto the cart, pawed at her pocket, and pulled out a mango treat. Wrancor knew this was beyond normal. But when the wallaby and Adrienne put their foreheads together for a few seconds and he let her pet him, his suspicions went full flare.

Adrienne's further carelessness happened at two in the morning. Although she knew there was a malevolent traveler somewhere in the world, she had no idea that he had been sitting thirty feet away when she was telling the wallaby how cute he was. She had decided to go back to Uluru and gaze at the stars from the top of the rock, and have a longer visit with the wallabies. Wrancor, who pretended to be sleeping for his companion's sake, was actually outside waiting. He was hovering behind a tree a few yards from the hotel. He had a direct view of Adrienne's room. He saw her leave through the roof.

In an instant he was back in his body and texting: Send a team to Ayers Rock Resort, Room 211. ASAP!!!

The next morning Adrienne went out hiking and climbing for the better part of the day with a group of college students. She was tired when she got back and went to her room for a rest.

Two men and a dog arrived by helicopter the same day. Neither of the men liked Wrancor. They could never figure out why Bayne pampered him. To them, he was a smug, puke of a weasel. They had no idea about his special abilities. Despite their disdain, they followed Bayne's orders. They knocked on the door of 211.

Wrancor answered.

"The boss said you needed us."

"I'll be back in a few minutes," Wrancor told Brandy. "I've got a business matter that I have to take care of." He came out on the walkway and closed the door behind him.

"We're going to do an abduction. Room 119. It is an older woman and she's pretty small. Shouldn't be much trouble. Leave the dog back at the helicopter. I want this done as quiet as possible, no commotion, no witnesses. Grab your bolt cutters and a stun gun."

After fetching their equipment, they joined Wrancor outside room 119. He clicked the knocker. The two other men plastered themselves against the wall on either side of the door.

Adrienne didn't leave her body to check outside. Instead, she opened the door just a crack. She at least left the safety chain attached. "Can I help you?"

"Good afternoon," Wrancor said. He smiled and sounded his charming best. "My girlfriend and I couldn't help noticing you were by yourself on this trip. We were wondering if you would like to join us for dinner this evening in the main dining room?"

"That might be possible," she said. "When were you thinking?"

"Say at seven o'clock?"

Adrienne, who was usually suspicious by nature had let her guard down this trip. After all, she thought, I'm in the middle of nowhere, not a lot of dangerous people about, just a bunch of casual tourists, and some wallabies.

"And whom, may I ask, shall I be having dinner with?"

"Let me give you my card," Wrancor answered.

He took a card from his wallet and handed it to Adrienne. When she opened the door a crack more and reached for the card, Wrancor grabbed her wrist and wrenched her arm through the opening. On cue, one of the henchmen shocked her on the side of her neck with the handheld taser. The other man snapped the safety chain with the bolt cutters. All three of them poured into her room closing the door behind them. It was over in seconds without a sound. Wrancor was strong and fast. He was clasping both of her wrists behind her back while one of the others cinched them together with plastic zip ties.

Wrancor threw her down on her bed.

Adrienne was slow to recover from the taser. It took a few seconds before she was able to sit up.

"Wait outside." Wrancor pointed toward the door. The two underlings obeyed his order.

"I always thought there were others out there like myself, but I wasn't sure until last night," Wrancor told her.

"What do you mean?" Adrienne slowly stretched her shoulders trying to regain her equilibrium and shake off the effects of the stun gun.

"You know. Last night when you went back out to the rock and had a bit of a sit down with the wallabies. I followed at a safe distance."

Adrienne didn't utter a word.

"Not very talkative this afternoon. Very well. Here are your options. You can come quietly with me and you will be treated respectfully. Or, you can resist and I'll give you a little something to put you to sleep. You could take off, but then my associates here will simply take your body, and you will have to follow them. That would be exhausting now, wouldn't it? You have to come back sometime, you know, eating, drinking, all that stuff. Can you even find your body if it's been moved? It's up to you."

"Followed me?" Adrienne tried to sound as naïve as possible.

"Yeah, you know…up, up, and away." Wrancor made a zooming motion with his arm.

Adrienne had to think fast. She realized this must be the dark traveler. Although the odds that he would be here were beyond calculation, here he was.

I better come up with a plan and fast, she thought.

She decided to go with surprise and fake innocence.

"You can travel too?" asked Adrienne. "Are there others? I have looked for years hoping to find someone but never have. I assumed I was alone."

"Well, now you know there is at least one more."

"So why you are treating me like this?" she asked. She lifted her bound hands. "I haven't done anything to you."

"As I said, you will be treated with respect if you come quietly."

"Go where? You're kidnapping me? I'm not of value to anyone. No one is going to pay a ransom for me. I don't have a family or money. I'm just a freelance journalist who does specials on animals. I don't get it."

"Really? Well, there is someone who wants to meet you. He'll think you are extremely valuable. All you say may be true, but I'm going to let him decide that."

Wrancor stuck his head outside and motioned for the men to come back into the room. "Get everything, bags, clothes, purse, phone, everything."

* * *

The two guards patrolling the front door of the ranch house snapped to full alert when Bayne's Mercedes pulled into the driveway. Adrienne was sitting on a leather sofa in the great room. Exposed beams held the vaulted ceiling aloft high above an enormous fieldstone fireplace. Windows framed with thick rough sawn timber faced the south, allowing streams of the sun to light up the dark-stained bamboo floor. She knew by the reactions of her guards when Bayne walked in, that this was the man who pulled the strings. He sat in the chair next to hers and stared at her. He was accompanied by a large Rhodesian Ridgeback.

"Sit, Cerberus," he commanded.

The dog sat upright to the side of the man's chair. His muscles were highlighted through his tawny hide.

Adrienne realized both man and dog were studying her. At barely five feet tall and lithe, she could be mistaken for a girl. However, her once raven black hair was now streaked with gray and the intelligence that could not be hidden in her large brown eyes revealed a wisdom that only comes with age. Despite her attempts to keep her emotions under total control, a great deal of anger was swimming in those eyes today.

"My name is Bayne. I trust you have been treated satisfactorily."

"Is that your first name or last name?" Adrienne asked.

She studied him as well. His face was clean-shaven and so was his head, not a wisp of hair anywhere. He was average height and stylishly trim, and she noted his linen suit and leather shoes didn't come from a department store. She couldn't help but observe the long jagged scar wandering down the side of his neck.

"First, last, does it matter? And what is your name?" he asked.

"I assume you've seen my driver's license."

He smiled. "Yes, one Brenda Harcourt, but I want to know if that's who you really are. I want to know *what* you really are."

During her captivity, Adrienne had been preparing for this meeting. She wanted to find out a few things as well. "As you said, my name is Brenda Harcourt. I'm a blogger and freelance journalist. You can check out my website at brendasanimalworld.com. You already know I can travel like your boy Colton, I believe his name is. I'm assuming you are curious about me and that's why I have been kidnapped."

"He's not my 'boy,' he's my associate. And kidnapped is such a strong word."

Adrienne pointed to the dogs and the guards outside the window. She also lifted her pants leg and pointed to the electric shock anklet. "Seems an appropriate term to me."

"Well, we can't have you leaving just yet."

"To answer your question," Adrienne continued. "I can't complain about the food and the bed is comfortable. Your dogs don't like me, however."

Bayne smiled. "It's their training you see. Now tell me, are there more out there like you?" he asked.

Item one, thought Adrienne: *He doesn't know how many of us there are.*

"I didn't know there was anyone else like me until three days ago," she said.

Bayne laughed, not a happy laugh, but a subdued, quiet, snickering laugh. "You don't lie very well. You know of at least one other."

"I do?" Adrienne asked.

"Yesterday you smiled and whispered, 'she knows.'"

"I don't remember saying that. I must have been dreaming."

"About who, I wonder?" Bayne asked.

Adrienne steered the conversation in a different direction. "You obviously know I can travel. I only do it when I really want to be with animals. It tires me greatly and I've come to believe traveling makes me age faster. It weakens me and causes me pain. So, I do it sparingly. What I haven't figured out is what you want with me."

Bayne rose from his chair and walked to the windows.

"Let me tell you a little story."

He drew a cigar out of his inner coat pocket, snipped off the end, and lit it with his gold plated lighter.

"Years ago there was an old man who lived here. I came to discover he had abilities similar to yours. At that time, I worked for someone of considerable wealth named Newsome. I was loyal, worked hard, and gained his trust. He and the old man used those abilities to their advantage. One day, however, the old man went out *traveling* and never came back. That was when I found out my employer was the legal guardian of a young boy named Colton Wrancor. Newsome died just before Colton entered his teens. A tragic death, I assure you. Guardianship was transferred to me. I have treated Colton like a son ever since. When he traveled I would make sure he told me all about it, just like he did for Newsome. I have nurtured his talent and his loyalty. I also heard a tale of a book, a special book that held the secrets of a group of people called *the astral*. My former employer believed that in the right hands the owner of this book would possess unheard-of power."

Item two, she thought: *He has heard rumors about the book but isn't sure it exists.*

Item three: *My cover story might work.*

"Mr. Bayne, I'm assuming it's Mister. I was also a child when I discovered I could travel outside my body. For me, it has always been about the animals. As I said before, I never told anyone. Well, I tried to tell my parents, but they assumed I had an overactive imagination. When I got a little older and tried to show them, they became frightened. They threatened to send me to a psychiatrist. That's when I stopped trying to convince them. For years I looked for others who were like me, hoped they were out there but I never found anyone. So, as I said, I have always believed I was alone. You're talking about things I know nothing about."

"Maybe I could believe you, but what kind of connections does a person have, that owns a phone that self destructs?"

"Did you do something to my phone?" She tried to sound shocked and outraged.

"When we tried opening it, the memory chip did more than a password blackout," Bayne answered. "Some kind of melting happened in the circuitry."

"That's not possible. Can I see it?"

Bayne pulled Adrienne's phone from his pocket and handed it to her. Twice she tried turning it on, both times acting like she was frustrated it wouldn't work. In her mind, however, she was delighted. Her phone was not only set to wipe all memory and history if it was in the wrong hands but before it disabled itself and fried the chip, it sent out a secret distress text to Arthur with latitude and longitude coordinates.

There was hope.

"I can't believe you wrecked my phone. It had tons of important information."

"I am suspecting you might be an accomplished actress Miss Harcourt, or whatever your name is. That phone was set to destroy itself and we both know it. However, let us get to the real reason I am here and the real reason you're still alive. I think you should consider working for me."

"Doing what exactly?"

"I am in the information business. I avail myself to knowledge that people pay for. Sometimes they pay to get the information, other times they pay to keep it a secret. I am sure you can see how someone with your talents would be extremely valuable in such an enterprise."

"So, you're a blackmailer and a spy, as well as a kidnapper."

"I like to think of myself as an arbiter of information, a dealer in the currency of valuable knowledge."

"And kidnapping is your normal method of recruitment?"

"Still such a strong word."

"It looks to me like you already have someone doing this work for you. Why would you need me?" she asked.

"Colton has his talents, yes. But two are always better than one."

"And if I don't?"

Bayne walked to the door. He turned back toward her before he left, took a long pull on his cigar, and blew out a slow, wispy cloud of smoke. "I'll let you sit on that thought for a day or two. It will give you time to think of the possibilities that await; especially the possibilities if you say no."

* * *

Back on the 87th floor of his Eureka Tower fortress, Bayne got online and searched out brendasanimalworld.com. There were archived weekly blogs going back six years. They were all about animals and contained extraordinary insights into their behavior. The site also had hundreds of photos, a brief bio, and contact info for anyone who wanted to hire her for freelance writing or photography. *Maybe she is Brenda Harcourt*, he thought to himself. *Or, maybe it is an elaborate cover. Either way, I am either going to use her or break her.*

Then he had a hunch and sent a text to his tech guy:

DO A SEARCH OF ANIMAL ACTIVITY THAT SEEMS

IMPOSSIBLE

Chapter 8
Marlboro Man

There was a ding on Dr. Armitauge's computer.

A new email simply read, "Gabriel got in. Video attached."

Dr. Armitauge clicked the icon for a specialized program of his design. It had an enhancement feature so unique it was the only one in existence. He opened the file and watched the recording three times. He was convinced after just one viewing that a silverback couldn't figure out locks but he couldn't help but watch again. The faint, heat wave-like blurs were not visible on every frame but there was no mistake that the gorilla was patting the invisible wave on the head and the elephant was rubbing her trunk on the side of it.

You know. But where are you?

The doctor called Francis once again. "She's out."

"Do you know who it is?" asked Francis.

"No. I'm sending Brandt. We are going to assume she is local. We have to find her before they do."

"Positive it's a girl?"

"Has to be," Arthur Armitauge answered. "If it's not, then we know nothing."

"That should be easy then. There are three million people in the Park City metro area. Knowing it's a girl cuts it down to one point five."

"I'll be doing nothing else but concentrating on how to draw her out and keep her safe. In the meantime please keep your sarcasm to yourself. It doesn't suit you and it doesn't help."

"Sorry Arthur, it just seems hopeless."

"Actually, Francis, we should have new hope. Twenty-four hours ago we knew nothing. Today, that is no longer true."

"What about Adrienne?"

"Nothing yet. I sent Boyd and Malek. They took Riga with them. We're going to find her."

* * *

"Oh my God Kita, you can't believe all the stuff I thought up last night," Amanda whispered. "There is so much we can do." She was just short of hopping with excitement when Kita joined her at the bus stop.

"What do you mean things 'we' can do?" Kita asked.

"We're in this together aren't we?"

"I guess we are."

"Do you realize all the secrets we can find out about people? Why, we could have a gossip blog that would always be dead on. We could drive Longstream crazy and he wouldn't even know where it was coming from. We could see what Miss Ober and Mr. Quade are really up to. We could . . ."

"Stop. I don't want to know what they're *really* up to."

"But —"

"I learned something last night," interrupted Kita.

"What?"

Kita told her about her conversation with Mtotah.

"Others? A school? Watchers? This is getting huge," Amanda said. "Maybe it has to do with other dimensions?"

"What?"

"Scientists think there are dimensions we can't see but they're right here in the same space we're in. Maybe that's what you travel through."

"I don't know about all that but there is something else that I can't quite explain."

"What?"

"It's a feeling. It's real strong inside me. I've never felt anything like it before. I got scared last night when Mtotah told me about the others. I feel that I'm only supposed to do this traveling for good things; that something bad might happen if I do it for bad things. Like maybe this whole thing might be dangerous."

"What kind of dangerous?"

"I don't know but the more I thought about it last night, the more worried I became."

"I'll put my scheming on hold then," Amanda said. "For a while anyway."

"There's something else."

"What?"

"My body hurts when I've come back from traveling. Maybe something happens to me when I travel."

"Maybe your right. You better lay low for a while until we get this figured out."

Kita's decision to do nothing to Ben Longstreet lasted less than five minutes into her first-hour science class. Mr. Granlund had a nasty protocol when he passed tests back. He handed them back in order, from best to worse. As always, Amanda got hers first. Kita was fourth from last.

"Hey Squat, figure it out yet?" Longstreet hissed.

"Figured what out, Your Dampness?" Kita sneered back.

"Look at problem number three. I knew you were an alien."

All the kids in the class turned their papers to problem number three. Harold Wartworth and Sandra Loder snickered. Amanda didn't. She pointed to Kita's answer. Number three was a Punnett Square problem about hair color. Kita got the problem correct so she couldn't figure out what Longstreet thought was so funny. Then she saw where Amanda was pointing and the realization hit her.

It hit her hard.

She started shaking but worked fiercely to control it. In seconds, tears welled up in her eyes. Kita had never cried in public. She wasn't about to start now. Two parents with blonde hair can't have a black-haired child. Stacy and Mike Tenzio were as blonde as they come.

"There's something about *your* Punnett Square, I don't understand," said Amanda. She turned toward Longstreet.

"Oh yeah, what's that?" he asked.

"How can two humans produce a dirt-bag?"

The class erupted in laughter, and the attention was taken away from Kita. She walked to the front of the room and obtained permission from Mr. Granlund to go see the nurse.

After class, Amanda went straight to the nurse's office.

"Can I help you?" Mrs. Valentine asked.

Mrs. V had been the school nurse forever. Everybody liked her because she was always nice and she never accused anyone of faking it, even when she knew they were. She also kept an endless supply of Hershey's Kisses in her bottom left drawer. "In case of emergencies," she'd told Amanda one day.

"Can I see Kita," Amanda asked.

"You can look in on her if you'd like. She's just resting."

Amanda slipped behind the curtain and sat next to Kita on the blue, vinyl cot. Kita's eyes were red and swollen. She sat up and Amanda held her.

"I didn't know you didn't know," Amanda said.

"Did you know?" Kita asked.

"No one told me or anything, but I figured it out in fourth grade when I read a book about heredity. I thought it would be obvious to you too, and that you already knew."

"I didn't. And besides, I'm so busy trying to memorize this stuff I never stop to think what it means."

"I'm sorry," Amanda said again.

"Don't be. I'll be alright. I'm going to stay here for a while longer though."

"Okay."

"Make sure you have a good view of Longstream at lunch," Kita said. "It might be good."

Amanda looked at Kita and smiled. "You going to do something?"

"Just watch."

"What about the danger thing?"

"I don't care," Kita answered. "He's going to pay."

On pleasant days, the students of Alkorn Heights Middle School got to eat their lunches outside. Longstreet, Wartworth, and Spencer Kelm always hogged the table that was under the tree farthest from the cafeteria door. Amanda sat a few tables away nibbling a ham and Swiss on rye.

She never heard them coming.

Barney, two shepherds, and a Rottweiler were on a beeline for Longstreet's table. When they were only a few feet away, all four started barking at him. Wartworth and Kelm scattered and Longstreet found himself alone and surrounded by four very large dogs.

"Get away from me you crazy dogs!" he shouted.

They held their places. Deep, menacing growls rumbled through their exposed teeth.

"Scram!" Longstreet shouted, waving his arms.

Three of the dogs pounced at once. The two shepherds grabbed the cuffs of his jeans and pulled him down so fast his butt hit the ground in a solid thud. The Rottweiler went for his shirt at his shoulder. Despite his screaming and squirming, the dogs pulled in opposite directions and held him in place. Then Barney bit down on Longstreet's backpack. He shook it and tore it open. A pack of cigarettes spilled out for all to see, including Mr. Connors, the lunch area supervisor. Then, in seconds, the dogs were gone. Twenty or so people had gathered in a circle watching Longstreet try to compose himself. He grabbed his backpack and hurried back toward the school doors with his two flunkies close behind.

"Wait!" shouted Mr. Connors. He was holding Longstreet's cigarette pack in the air. "I think you forgot something."

Longstreet looked back. "Those aren't mine," he answered.

Mr. Connors smiled. "Oh, just kind of magically fell out of your backpack did they? Come with me, Longstreet. We're going to the office."

"Wow!" Amanda whispered to herself.

The next thing she knew, Kita was standing beside her.

"What do you think?" she asked.

"That was seriously awesome!" Amanda said. "How did you know he smoked?"

"Can't you smell it on him when we get on the bus?"

"Never thought about it."

"That should get him out of our hair for a few days at least."

"There's something you didn't plan on though," Amanda said.

"What?"

"I'm pretty sure quite a few people got the whole thing on their phones."

Kita looked around at all the spectators. She hung her head.

"You're right," she said. "I never thought about that."

And Amanda was right. In less than two hours the entire internet was lit up with multiple postings and hundreds of views of four dogs harassing a boy trying to eat his school lunch.

* * *

Oliver Brandt was thirty-two years old and exactly a half-inch shorter than six feet. He worked hard at remaining non-descript. His short brown hair was always neat and he never allowed himself even a day's worth of facial hair. He wore bland colored, semi-loose fitting clothing to appear as average as possible, and to hide the fact that his body was fit to the extreme. He never walked anywhere fast, but to the casual observer, he at least looked like a man who knew where he was headed. By pure chance, he was sitting in his car marking up a map of the locations of all the schools in the Park City metropolitan area when he happened to notice four dogs, side by side, all walking in the same direction. Their course never wavered. It was as if they were on a mission.

Oliver hopped out of his car and followed at a brisk pace. He didn't want to run, but he didn't want to lose them either. Three blocks ahead they turned into an alley. They stayed in formation. He quickened his pace even more. When he reached the alley they were out of sight. He ran. He caught a glimpse of them on the far side of a park. They were running. He tracked the exact path the dogs had taken. When he crossed the park he heard a commotion of some kind outside a school across the street. He moved closer to get a better look. Kids were outside eating their lunches. Closer to the building, a larger group of kids were standing and a man was holding up a pack of cigarettes. The dogs were nowhere to be seen. He scanned all directions. Nothing. He noticed a few of the students looking at each other's phones.

"That was weird," Brandt whispered to no one.

Chapter 9
A Baby in a Box

Kita's mom kept glancing her way. "You're awful quiet tonight," she said.

Kita pushed her potatoes around on her plate, stared at the swirl they made but did not respond.

The Tenzios made it a priority to have dinner together as many evenings as they could. Most of those dinners were alive with conversations about the activities of the day and Kita was usually the most talkative of the four.

Not tonight.

"Are you alright?" asked Mike. "You don't look well."

She still didn't answer. She didn't know how to answer. She was bitterly hurt that her parents had never told her the truth. It felt like a giant bruise all over her body, inside and out.

"I know she was in the nurse's office today," Zach announced.

"How would you know that?" asked Stacy.

"Brenda Teffren saw her coming out during lunch."

"Is that true Kita?" Stacy asked with obvious concern in her voice.

Kita looked up at her mom. Tears leaked out the corners of her eyes.

"Oh honey, what's the matter?" asked Stacy.

Kita could hold it in no longer. Her tears broke out into full-blown crying.

"Why didn't you tell me?" Kita said, choking out the words between sobs.

"Tell you what dear?" Stacy asked. She looked over at her husband with a bit of alarm.

Kita got herself together enough to speak. "That I'm adopted."

"I knew it!" exclaimed Zach. He pointed an accusing finger at her. "I knew you were too dumb to be related to me."

Kita threw her glass at Zach's head. He ducked but it grazed his ear and most of the milk ended up on his shirt.

"Zach, to your room. Now!" Mike Tenzio commanded. "And if you know what is good for you, you'll go quickly, and not allow another word to come out of your mouth! You stay in that room until I come up there!"

Zach grumbled all the way up the stairs.

Stacy came over and held Kita in her arms. Kita didn't push her away but she didn't hug back either.

"Let's go into the other room," Mike suggested.

All three sat on the sofa with Kita in the middle.

Mike started the conversation. "When you were young your mom and I talked back and forth many times if we should tell you. We decided we would wait and see if you would ask. As time went on we kept talking about it and we kept waiting. It never seemed like the time was right and . . ."

"Why did you wait?"

"Most of the time, when children are adopted, something is known about the birth parents," Stacy broke in. "So the children are usually told in case they have questions about their biological parents. Or, sometimes they even want to meet them. Although, that usually doesn't happen until they get older. But we know absolutely nothing about your birth parents."

"Why not?" asked Kita trying to quiet down her crying.

Mike handed her a box of tissues. She wiped her cheeks and blew her nose.

"You were placed on the altar of a church in San Antonio early on a Sunday morning. A priest found you when he was preparing for the first service of the day; just a baby in a cardboard box. There was a note pinned to your blanket."

"What did it say?"

"All it said was, 'Her name is Kita.' Then you were taken to a hospital and the doctors determined you were only a day or two old."

"But you're from Minnesota, how did you know about me way up here?"

"There is an agency in San Antonio called Homes for Infants. They're an orphanage that specializes in newborns. The director at the time was your great aunt Susan. She knew we were interested in adopting a girl. You were in my arms two days later. We waited over a year to see if anyone would come forward to claim you. When they didn't we made the adoption official."

"How did you find out about this?" Mike asked.

"I figured it out in science class. We've been studying heredity and hair color."

"Ah, the Punnett Square," Stacy sighed.

"It's a bad way to find out," Kita told them.

"We're so sorry Kita. And you are right. It is a bad way to find out. It's obvious now we didn't handle this the right way." Stacy hugged Kita again and mouthed, 'Say something,' to Mike.

"The fact you're adopted doesn't change anything about how we love you. I have loved you since the first time I snuggled my nose in your neck. You are *my* daughter, Kita. And nothing will ever change that," Mike said.

"Do you love me the same way you love Zach?"

They didn't answer immediately and it alarmed Kita. She wrenched herself from her mother's grip, stood up, and planted her hands on her hips.

"I thought so!" she declared.

Her parents looked at each other. Stacy nodded.

"There is something else you need to know Kita," said Mike in a calm steady voice.

"What?"

"Before I tell you, you are going to have to make the biggest and strongest promise of your life. And keep it a secret for three years. Think you can do that?"

She waited and thought some before she answered. She was trying to figure out what could be such a big secret that she had to keep it for three years. Finally, she relented. "I promise."

"Zach is adopted too, and he doesn't know either. He just happened to turn out blonde like us."

Kita was dumbfounded.

"Why haven't you told him?" she asked.

"We promised his birth mother we would not tell him until he was eighteen. We actually have a letter from her that we will give him on his eighteenth birthday."

Kita sat back down. All her angry steam slowly wisped away.

"You see Kita," Stacy continued, "something is wrong with my body and I can't have children of my own. Your dad and I both knew we had love and a good home to give so we adopted. We love you both the same. In fact, I can't imagine if I had biological children that I could love them more than I love you two."

Then there was silence.

The three Tenzios allowed that silence to rest on them. They sunk back into the billowy cushions. Mike and Stacy wrapped their arms around her.

It was Mike who finally spoke.

"Does it bother you that you're adopted?" he asked.

"I don't know," said Kita. "I have to think about all this."

"I know," said Stacy. "You've got a lot to deal with today."

You don't know the half of it. Three days ago I was a semi-happy, almost normal kid. Now I can transport myself all over the place, talk to animals and I don't know who I really am. And Amanda thinks I might not even be human.

"A lot," Kita agreed.

"Can you forgive us?" Mike asked. "We aren't claiming we handled this completely right but it was done out of care."

"I forgive you," Kita answered.

"Any other questions you want to ask?" Stacy offered.

"Not right now but can I go over to Amanda's?"

"Sure. I suppose you are going to want to tell her," Mike said.

"She already knows. She figured it out before me?"

"She did?"

Kita explained in detail how events unfolded in science class that morning at school.

It was Stacy's turn to need tissues.

* * *

Amanda and Kita were sitting on a two-person swing on the Griffith's back patio.

"Did they tell you the truth?" she asked.

"Yes."

"And?"

Kita recounted her conversation with her parents making sure to avoid any mention of Zach.

"So maybe you're somehow related to this Adrienne," Amanda speculated.

"Yeah, maybe, but I'll never know," Kita sighed. "I don't even know if tomorrow is my real birthday."

"Speaking of birthday," said Amanda. "We got interrupted by that tiger yesterday. The puppy is for you I hope you know."

"Really. You actually got me a puppy? My parents are going to freak."

"They already know. I asked if it was okay before I did it. So, how do you want to meet your new puppy, as real Kita or *traveler* Kita."

"Real, but wait just one minute."

Kita raced home, took a piece of bacon out of the fridge, cut it into six pieces, and ran back to Amanda's. She wanted the introduction to be special.

The puppy hopped tiny hops and wagged her tail in a frenzy when the girls entered the garage. Amanda opened the kennel and the little amber haired fur ball stumbled out and started licking her hand. Kita walked over and scooped her up. She held one of the bacon pieces in her other hand. The puppy was all over it. One by one, Kita fed her new pet each bit of bacon. The puppy licked Kita's fingers furiously after she devoured the last piece.

"She'll love you forever now," said Amanda.

"It's the best present ever!" Kita said smiling.

"What are you going to name her?"

Kita raised the puppy up to her face and they rubbed noses. There was a slender streak down the puppy's front that was curlier than the rest of her hair. It was also a lighter shade, truly golden.

"I'm going to name her Goldilocks. Goldie for short."

That night, Barney slept on the floor in front of Kita's bed like he did every night. However, Kita and Goldie cuddled under the covers until they both fell asleep.

Chapter 10
Thirteen Candles and a Silo

"Happy Birthday!" Stacy and Mike called out when Kita came through the saloon-style doors to the kitchen.

Zach also wished her a happy birthday, with the enthusiasm of someone who had just been grounded for the weekend.

In the middle of the kitchen island was a chocolate cake with thirteen candles waiting to be lit. Chocolate cake for breakfast was Kita's favorite birthday tradition. She was holding Goldie in her arms and Barney followed close behind.

"I see Amanda gave you your present early," Mike said.

"Did you name her yet?" Stacy asked.

"Goldie."

"Oh boy, another animal around here," Zach complained. "We've got rabbits, birds, guinea pigs, turtles, and now two dogs. It's a regular zoo around here."

Kita ignored him.

They moved to the living room to open presents. Mike gave her a cushioned bed for Goldie. A delicate necklace adorned with a jeweled *K* in a fancy box was from her mom and Zach gave her a bag of Starburst.

The festivities were interrupted by a knock on the back door. It was Amanda.

"Hi everybody," she said.

"Hi Amanda," they all called back.

"Have you watched the news this morning?" Amanda asked trying to sound casual. "They found that gorilla that escaped from the zoo."

Kita hurried back to the kitchen and turned on the television.

"We're coming to you live," the reporter announced. "As you can see behind me, Elliot the silverback from Capitol Zoo has been located. Officials here are trying to contain the situation."

The camera changed its focus to the scene behind the reporter. Elliot was atop a huge blue silo. It was surrounded by three sheriff's vehicles, two pick-up trucks, and an oversized van from the zoo. A helicopter buzzed overhead. It was *King Kong* all over again.

"I have the head zoo administrator here," the reporter continued. "Tell us, Ms. Smythe, what exactly is the current status?"

"The owner of this farm came upon Elliot this morning. Evidently, he was eating some carrots and potatoes that were meant for the pigs. He was startled and instead of running off, he went up the ladder to the top of the silo."

"How do you plan on getting him down?" asked the reporter.

"We're not sure about that yet," Connie Smythe answered. "We don't want to hurt him and obviously we don't want anyone getting hurt as we bring him in."

"There you have it, folks. Reporting live from Estenson, this is April Hunnicut."

Kita was horrified. She remembered the words of Saamradi about not being captured alive. The thought of Mahshando getting killed was like a knife twisting in her heart. She grabbed Amanda's hand.

"Is it okay if Kita comes over for a couple of minutes?" asked Amanda. "I know you guys are going to the theater later. This shouldn't take that long."

"Sure," Stacy said.

The girls left as casual as could be but once outside they sprinted to Amanda's room.

"I thought you would want to help your friend."

"I do," said Kita, "but I don't know where this Estenson is."

Amanda hit the space bar on her laptop. Google Maps was already up. A red pin flagged Estenson, a small town forty-five miles southwest of Alkorn Heights.

"Which way is that from here?" asked Kita.

"Man you really do need me," Amanda said. "It's that way." She pointed to the wall behind her bed. "I can't believe you can fly all over the place and don't know your directions."

"I'm going to learn them now," she answered.

Kita laid on the bed. "Thanks for getting me," she said.

"I'll wait here and make sure no one comes in," said Amanda. "Now go!"

Kita rocketed through the roof and went speeding southwest. In seconds, dense neighborhoods gave way to open spaces. She went past two towns and only moments later saw a water tower that looked like a hot air balloon. ESTENSON was painted on the side. She stopped and hovered above the top and scanned . . . nothing. Then she used her zoom vision. There he was, only a few miles away. Before he took his next breath, she was at his side.

"Mahshando, it's me," she said.

"You have come."

"I want to help you."

"How? I'm not going back into the cage."

"You can't stay up here forever," she said.

"I'd rather die here than go back."

"Why did you climb up here? Why didn't you keep running when you saw the farmer?"

"High ground was my first thought. Although this isn't ground." He pounded the top of the silo.

"They won't kill you," Kita said. "You're too valuable. Plus, there are cameras now."

"Cameras?" asked Mahshando.

"We don't have time for that now," Kita said. "We have to get you out of here."

She gazed in all directions. To the west, she saw a narrow river bordering the far side of a field. On the other side of the river was a giant wooded area edged by a ravine. It led to a rocky outcrop that climbed upwards for hundreds of feet. No vehicle would be able to follow.

"I have an idea," Kita said pointing to the hopeful escape route. "Slide down the ladder as fast as you can. Then, follow me."

Mahshando swung his body around and slid down the ladder like it was a fire pole. Kita was waiting for him at the bottom. There was an excited flurry of activity as people tried to react to the sudden change in the situation. They were too slow. Their nets, and ropes, and traps were not at the ready. None of the deputies seemed too interested in confronting a four hundred pound gorilla either.

Mahshando ran as fast as he could with Kita leading the way. They cleared the field and were only yards from the river when the loud crack of a rifle rippled through the air.

"Ughh," Mahshando groaned.

"Nooooo!" Kita screamed. Only Mahshando heard her cries.

"Are you hit?" she asked.

"Keep running. It's no worse than a snake bite," he said.

But he slowed when they reached the water. On the far side, he collapsed face first in the mossy bank. A dart was firmly lodged in his right shoulder.

Kita knelt at his side. "Can you hear me?" she pleaded.

The was no answer.

Two trucks raced across the field toward them.

"I hate you! I hate you! I hate you!" Kita screamed as the men loaded Mahshando in the back of the biggest truck.

She hopped on the truck and spoke into Mahshando's ear.

"This isn't over," she told him.

He turned his head groggily toward her. She hoped he heard.

* * *

"They got him," Kita said when she opened her eyes.

"Is he alive?" Amanda asked.

"Yeah. They used a drug dart."

"You don't look so good," Amanda said. "Are you all right?"

"I don't know. I feel really tired and my body doesn't feel right; kind of aches."

"Maybe traveling really does do something to you," Amanda suggested.

"Maybe."

The pain of defeat hung in the room like a drenching vapor clinging to the girls in a depressing mist.

* * *

Oliver Brandt's ringtone was Big Ben from London. He never spoke when he pushed the green phone icon, only listened.

"Did you see the footage about the gorilla?" It was Dr. Armitauge on the other end.

"Yes."

"I want you to go and meet the sheriff in that town."

"What do you want me to ask him?"

"See if you can get a copy of the video from the helicopter. I noticed it was from law enforcement, not a television crew."

"Very well. There is one other thing I think I should mention," said Brandt.

"Yes?"

"I saw a pack of dogs yesterday, four of them. It was almost like they were walking in a formation of some kind. I followed them on foot. I thought they were headed to a school. When I got there they were gone."

"How were they walking?"

"Two by two, no dog in the front."

"Anything else?"

"It looked like there had been a scene of some kind. A teacher was holding up a pack of cigarettes. I'm not sure if the dogs were part of it or not."

"What is the name of the school?"

"Alkorn Heights Middle School."

"I will see what I can find out about that. You go see the sheriff at Estenson."

"On my way," Brandt said.

Within minutes he was driving out of Park City, heading southwest.

* * *

Dr. Arthur Armitauge went online and searched: Alkorn Heights Middle School, dogs, cigarettes, and the date. There were five videos to choose from. Three of them clearly showed four dogs in a coordinated effort going after a boy. One video showed more of the crowd reactions and everyone grabbing for their phones. One of them, however, focused for a few seconds on a girl with copper hair and oversized glasses sitting on a table. She was watching the events like everyone else but she was different. She sat calm and steady; almost like it wasn't a surprise to her. He turned on his enhancement software. He watched it again. He saw it: a faint distortion wave next to the dog shaking the backpack.

"There you are," he whispered.

He captured a still shot of the girl with the copper hair and texted it to Brandt: Forget Estenson, go back to Park City. Find this girl. She's at the school where you saw the dogs.

Chapter 11
The Preserve

"Look at what I found last night," Amanda said. The girls were sitting next to each other on the bus and Amanda was pointing to her phone. The picture on the screen was of a lion lounging under a mesquite tree.

"What is it?" Kita asked.

"It's called the Aegis Preserve. They make a home for large animals that cannot be introduced back to the wild. Their motto is: *Freeing Animals One Cage at a Time.* They own sixty-four square miles of land so the animals can roam all over the place."

Kita sat up straighter. She grabbed the phone from Amanda and scrolled through more images of Aegis. She smiled. Then she laughed. Then she hugged Amanda. "Where is this place? We have to get Mahshando there."

"I know, right. It's in the far southwest part of Arizona."

Kita's shoulders slumped. "Arizona? I can't lead him all the way down to Arizona."

"I know that. That is not how we're going to get him there. We are going to start a *Free Elliot* campaign. We'll make posters for school, put a video on YouTube, and a post on Face book. I've already started a GoFundMe account. We'll buy Elliot from the zoo and ship him to the preserve."

"How much will it cost?"

"I don't know but we're going to find out and we're starting today. Mom agreed to take us to the zoo after school."

"You're brilliant Amanda," Kita gushed.

"I know."

After seventh hour the girls hopped into the Griffith's car. Molly Griffith was slender, had straight auburn hair, and a thin nose like her daughter. Amanda would look like her if she didn't have spiked copper hair and big glasses. Molly Griffith owned a clothing and accessory boutique in downtown Park City. She'd taken the afternoon off.

"I think what you girls are doing is really great," Molly said. "I'm so proud of you for starting such a worthy cause."

The girls smiled.

At the zoo, they took a direct path to Elliot's glass house. She and Amanda sat on a bench. Kita leaned back into Amanda's arms.

"What are you girls doing?" Molly asked.

"It's okay Mom. Kita just needs a short rest."

"I am so sorry they caught you," Kita told Mahshando once she was inside the glass.

"I can't be in here anymore. I am going to stop eating."

"Don't! I don't have time to explain it all but Amanda and I have a plan. That's her over there." Kita pointed to Amanda.

"Which one is her?"

"The one with the copper hair. Can't you tell I'm the other girl?"

"Your skin is a different color. And, I don't know how can you be in two places at the same time?"

"There is a physical me and a traveler me. Remember what Mtotah said."

"How come your eyes are closed over there?"

"I sort of sleep when I travel. I came here to tell you we're going to bring you to a good place. It might take us a little while but we're coming for you."

"What kind of a place?"

"A place with no cages. A place where no one can stare at you and where you can walk wherever you want. There are real trees and real grass and other gorillas too. Promise me you will eat and stay strong."

"If what you say is true, I will stay strong."

"It's true, I promise. Now, I need you to stand by the glass over by that sign and look sad."

"I am sad."

When Kita came back, Amanda handed her a tissue from her purse. Kita wiped tears from her cheeks.

"This seems a little strange?" said Molly. "Why are you crying, Kita?"

"I'll be okay, Mrs. Griffith. I'm just a little emotional about Elliot."

"Kita, you handle the video." Amanda handed her phone to Kita. Then she stood next to the pewter sign.

Mahshando was next to the glass, behind her, and to the right.

"Ready?"

"Ready," Kita said. She pushed *record*.

"Hi, my name is Amanda Griffith. I am at Capitol Zoo in front of the glass cage that holds Elliot the great silverback. You may have seen him in the news recently. Imagine if you were trapped in a tiny space with a fake tree, fake rocks, fake vines, rotten food, and no privacy. You'd want to escape too. I am here today to ask you to join me and free Elliot. Please find our GoFundMe page and type in FreeElliotCampaign. You can be part of a great cause to buy him from this zoo, have him transferred to a wonderful place where he can roam free, and have all the privacy he wants. Join us today!"

"That was great Amanda!" Kita exclaimed.

All three watched the video to make sure it was acceptable.

"Excellent dear," Molly said.

"Thanks, guys."

* * *

Mr. Rister, the principal, gave the girls permission to set up a table in the main foyer before and after school. He even contributed ten dollars to the cause. Amanda had made a colorful poster with a big photo of Elliot and put it on the wall behind them. A computer on the table played Amanda's video on a repeat loop. People started coming. Amanda and Kita told people to create a link on their Face book accounts and spread the word. Even Longstream and Warthog stopped by.

"So Squat, I see you're trying to free the relatives," he said with a vile snicker.

"Yeah," added Warthog. "I can see the resemblance."

Amanda grabbed Kita's arm and kept her from bolting out of her chair. "You see, Longstream," Amanda said, "we're trying to make room in the glass cage for *homo stupidus*. And we have the perfect candidate."

That garnered a few chuckles from the bystanders.

Ben Longstreet's ignorant remarks were the only negative response the girls encountered. By the second day, the whole thing had gone viral. The same television station that covered Elliot's capture sent out the same reporter to interview the girls. April Hunnicut was in her late twenties, had straight blonde hair, and green eyes. Her navy blue dress suit and pink silk shirt were professionally fitted. She wore high heels that raised her over six feet. The girls stood next to their table with the poster highlighted behind them.

"I am here this morning with Kita Tenzio and Amanda Griffith.

These two girls have started quite a stir with their Free Elliot Campaign. What gave you this idea girls?" April held the microphone in front of Amanda.

"When we saw the capture of Elliot on the news, we knew we had to do something," Amanda answered. "It is not right that such a majestic creature is kept in a cage."

"How much money has the campaign raised so far?"

"We're over $7,000.00."

"And how much does the zoo want for Elliot?"

"They won't tell us. They say he isn't for sale," said Kita. "But we're going to win."

"There you have it, folks. Two inspiring young girls fighting for animal freedom and a zoo that won't even entertain their offer. Reporting live from Alkorn Heights Middle School, this is April Hunnicut."

When the camera was off, April turned toward the girls. "This publicity will put some pressure on them," she said.

"Thank you, Ms. Hunnicut," the girls said in unison.

"Call me April. By the way, I contributed, and I had something made up for you at the station."

She pulled out twenty pages of stickers. Elliot's picture was on each sticker with, *I gave* inscribed at the bottom.

"Wow, these are great!" exclaimed Amanda.

Taking it all in, while leaning against a wall safely away from the action, was a man with fake press credentials. He stepped forward. He asked the girls if he could take their picture and ask them a few questions for a story he was doing for Animal Universe Magazine. They readily agreed. The man was Oliver Brandt.

Chapter 12

First Contact

Francis Armitauge answered his phone.

"We found her," Arthur said.

"Adrienne?"

"No. The girl. I will send you details when I know more. Wait 'til you see what she looks like."

"What about Adrienne?"

"Nothing yet."

"Find her Arthur."

"I'm trying but you know our only real hope is if she can find us."

"What do you want me to do?"

"Come to the island in case Boyd and Malek check-in. I'm going to Park City."

"Be careful Arthur."

"Always."

* * *

Dr. Arthur Armitauge was well past ninety years old. He still had hair and it still had random streaks of gray mixed in with all the white. A precisely trimmed mustache and goatee gave the illusion he was a few years younger. He was only five and a half feet tall and thinner now than he was as a young man. Still, his custom-tailored three-piece suit fit him to a tee. He held a slim leather briefcase in one hand and a pearl-handled walking stick was tucked under his other arm. He rang the Tenzio's doorbell at 6:30 pm sharp.

Mike Tenzio answered.

"Can I help you?" he asked.

"Good evening. Please excuse my interruption. My name is Dr. Arthur Armitauge. I was hoping I might have a word with you and your daughter about her Free Elliot campaign. I watched her on the news. I believe I might be able to help."

He handed a business card to Mike. It simply read:

Dr. Arthur Armitauge MD. PhD. PhD.

"I guess it would be all right," Mike said. He opened the door wider and placed the card in his shirt pocket. He led him to the front room. "Please have a chair. I'll go get Kita."

"Would your wife be able to join us as well?"

"I'll ask."

Mike found Stacy and Kita in the kitchen.

"Who was at the door?" Stacy asked.

"Some old guy, very dapper. He wants to talk to three of us about Kita's free the gorilla thing."

"It is Free Elliot," Kita reminded him.

"Yeah. That's what I meant."

"Let's go see what he has to say," Stacy said.

When the three of them returned to the front room, Dr. Armitauge was still standing. He introduced himself, first to Stacy and then Kita.

"You caught my attention on the news Miss Tenzio and I must say I am quite impressed."

"You can call me Kita."

"Very well then, Kita it is."

"My husband said you might be able to help Kita and Amanda with their campaign," Stacy said.

"I believe that may be so. But first, Kita, I was wondering if I might be permitted to ask you a couple of questions?" He focused his gaze on her.

"Sure."

"What gave you this freedom idea in the first place?"

"It was actually Amanda's idea. She found out about the Aegis Preserve after we saw Elliot captured on the news. She's brilliant with computers and social media. I'm just along because I love animals and I'm her friend."

"I see. And when was the first time you ever saw Elliot?"

Kita hesitated. "Well, I aah —"

"Remember honey you saw him at the zoo when you were five," Stacy said.

"Oh yeah. That's right. I forgot all about that," Kita lied. She looked into Dr. Armitauge's eyes. They seemed kind, but she was convinced he knew she was keeping a secret.

Next, he pulled an envelope out of his briefcase. He opened it and took out a letter and handed it to Kita.

"Can you make any sense of this?" he asked.

Kita looked at the letter. The symbols looked like words, but they were in a language she had never seen before.

"I don't think so." She handed the letter back.

Dr. Armitauge frowned. "That's too bad because it is from a woman named Adrienne. I was hoping you may have heard of her."

Kita said nothing. She stared at Dr. Armitauge and went into a full-blown panic. She willed herself to stay calm but her hands were twitching. She pushed her feet into the carpet as hard as she could to keep her legs from trembling.

"What's wrong?" Stacy asked. "Why are you shaking? Do you know someone named Adrienne?"

"No."

"Then why are you shaking?"

"I can't say." Kita's lips were quivering and she was tearing up.

"What's the big idea coming in here and scaring my daughter? I thought you said you were here about the gorilla." Mike Tenzio's voice was getting gruffer with each word. "What kind of doctor are you anyway? I think it's time you left."

"I am very sorry. I did not mean to frighten Kita. As far as what kind of doctor I am. First I became a medical doctor, a surgeon actually. Then, I got my first PhD. in quantum physics. My second PhD. is in ancient civilizations." He put the letter back in the case and stood to take his leave. "Before I leave please permit me to say one last thing." He turned and looked straight into Kita's eyes. "Kita, I know you want to know. I am the person who can answer your questions. You can trust your parents. I can see they love you very much. I will help you tell them."

"Okay. That is enough! Your talking crazy talk!" Mike shouted. "Out! Now!" He pointed to the door.

"As you wish. I can show myself out." He made a slight bow, collected his briefcase and walking stick, then turned toward the door.

"Wait."

It was Kita.

The doctor turned back and faced her.

"You say you will help me? Can you really help me?"

"I promise I will do everything in my power to help you and protect you."

"What in the world are you two talking about?" Stacy asked. "I don't like this. This conversation has just gotten really weird. Protect her from what?"

"May I sit?"

Mike's curiosity was stronger than his anger. He nodded toward the chair.

Dr. Armitauge faced Kita. "Do you want me to stay?"

"Yes."

"Before I start to explain things, I need Kita to try one more time. You will be able to read this letter but only if you wear this ring."

He held out a gold ring that looked primitive like it had been forged in an ancient fire. Three symbols were carved on the surface. Kita took the ring. It was too big for her fingers, so she slipped it on her thumb. She was amazed when the ring shrunk and hugged her thumb. She felt a surge of energy flow into her body. She was able to sense her real body and her astral body at the same time.

This is incredible.

Dr. Armitauge set the letter back on the table.

Kita stood over the table and examined the letter. The writing was now clear and she could read it easily.

My Dearest Child,

If you are reading this letter then three things have happened:

You have discovered you can travel, you have met Arthur, and I am either dead or being held somewhere against my will. You can trust Dr. Armitauge. He is very wise. Allow him to be your mentor. He will tell you who I am and answer all your other questions.

My greatest desire is that we meet, so I can hold you in my arms, and teach you many things you need to know.

Until then give Arthur a hug. He is an old man who has sacrificed much.

With all my love.

Adrienne

When Kita finished she walked over to Dr. Armitauge.

"Stand up please, Doctor."

He did. She threw her arms around him and hugged him tightly.

"My my, Kita what's all this?" he asked, patting her on the shoulder.

"She said you needed a hug."

Stacy and Mike were dumbfounded. They looked at each other, they looked at Kita, and they looked at the little old man in the three-piece suit. Stacy was the first to break out of their stupor.

"Who's the *she*?"

"Adrienne," Kita answered.

"I thought you said you don't know her?"

"I don't."

"Then what —?"

"I just read the letter," Kita said pointing to the letter still sitting on the table. "She wrote it to me."

"If you don't know each other, how in the world can she write a letter to you?" Stacy asked.

"We don't know each other, we just know each other exists."

"What?"

"Doctor," Kita said. "I think it's time for you to say something."

"Let's try something else before we get to how Adrienne knows about Kita," Dr. Armitauge suggested. "You can also read the letter without the ring."

"But when I looked at it before I put the ring on, it didn't make any sense."

"You can read it when you are in your other place."

"What other place?" Mike asked. "She's not going anywhere with you."

"It's okay dad." Kita took the ring off and set it on the table. She sensed an emptiness when it left her hand like she was losing energy.

She wished she could keep it on forever. She was unsure about traveling in front of her parents; not sure if she was ready for this. She looked over to the doctor for help.

"It's okay Kita. As I said, I will help you tell them."

Kita leaned in close to her mom. "Will you hold me for a few seconds?"

"Okay?"

Kita went limp, her eyes closed, and all her weight pushed into Stacy.

"What's happened to her?" Stacy asked, alarmed.

Dr. Armitauge held up his hand. "She is fine. She will be back in a moment."

"What do you mean, back?" Mike asked. He was still being sarcastic.

"If you will just give her a moment, we will explain all to you. Please trust me, and most importantly, trust her."

The doctor was right. Kita could read the letter as a traveler just like she could when she wore the ring.

Kita opened her eyes and sat up straight. "You were right."

"Whoa. Whoa. Whoa. This is nuts! What in the world is going on around here?" Mike asked.

Dr. Armitauge sat back down and Kita snuggled closer to her mom. She slid her hand into Stacy's, their fingers intertwining.

"Will you start please?" Kita asked. "You said you would help me tell them."

"Indeed I did."

Chapter 13

The Astral

Bayne was frustrated. He still wasn't sure what to make of the woman tucked away at his big house and he wasn't sure how he should proceed with her. A buzzing on his phone interrupted his pacing.

"What?" he shouted. "I've told you to text and never call."

"I did text a while ago but I thought this might be important. I sent a link to your email of a YouTube video from the U.S."

"I don't have time for some YouTube bullshit!" he screamed.

"You will want to see this one Sir. Remember, you wanted me to look up unusual animal activity."

Bayne clicked the space bar of his computer and clicked on the link in his email. He watched a video of four dogs opening a boy's backpack with a coordinated effort he knew was impossible. He watched it over and over looking for one thing in the crowd that seemed out of place. Then he saw it, a spike-haired, copper headed girl with oversized glasses sitting calm and still as if she wasn't watching anything unusual at all.

* * *

"Kita is an Astral," Dr. Armitauge began.

"An Astral?" Mike wondered out loud. He couldn't hide the extreme distaste from his tone.

"I am going to tell you things that are going to push your beliefs to the outer boundaries," the doctor continued. "Please bear with me and hear me out."

"We'll listen." She motioned for Mike to calm down.

"Kita has the ability to leave her physical body. She can travel anywhere she wants at incredible speed."

"What, like some astral-projection thing?" Mike asked.

"I have never been able to verify astral-projection as it is defined in science fiction and the fringe journals. They just talk about the mind traveling, which may be possible, I don't know. What Kita does is different. Her astral essence actually has a body. It's just not a physical one as we would think."

"Am I right Kita?"

"Yes."

Her parents had never given her a look more strange.

"She can also communicate with animals."

"What!?"

"Allow me to show you something. Watch carefully and tell me what you notice."

He opened his briefcase and slid out an iPad. He clicked an icon, then turned the screen so Kita and her parents could see. It was the unedited surveillance video of the breakout at the zoo. They watched Mahshando do his running charges that broke down his door. Then they watched as he trekked through the zoo sliding open every bolt he could. In awe, they viewed a parade of animals bowing and performing various gestures in front of the gorilla. Finally, they watched as the gorilla and a great elephant seemingly reached out to touch something in front of them.

"I thought they said the video system had been hacked by the activists," Stacy said. "How did you get this?"

"As you can see, there were no animal rights advocates that night.

As far as securing the video, I have a technical man in my employ who has some unusual abilities of his own. But tell me now, what did you notice?"

"I saw a gorilla somehow using mechanical reasoning. I didn't think that was possible," Mike said.

"At the end it looked like Elliot and that elephant were looking at the same thing. It almost looked like a heat wave." Stacy added.

"The heat wave is me," Kita said.

Everyone stared at her.

"I've seen it before. Amanda took a video of me the other day. We saw it then but not as clear as this."

"What are you talking about?" asked Mike. "There isn't anyone there."

"You are a very clever girl," said Dr. Armitauge. "But it is not exactly a heat wave. Even though your physical body is not present, your astral body does impact space. It creates a minor distortion. I had a special software developed that is able to enhance the distortion."

"Amanda and I were wondering what it was. So, I'm not in another dimension or something?" Kita asked.

"No. What made you think that?"

"It was Amanda's idea," answered Kita. "She knows all about dimensions and physics and stuff. I think she's probably a genius."

"I am looking forward to meeting her," Dr. Armitauge said.

"What in the world are you two talking about?" Mike interrupted. His voice was getting louder and rougher.

"Just hang on for one more second, Dad."

"So, your friend Amanda knows everything?"

"Yes."

"I think then it is your turn to talk."

Kita straightened up and turned to her mother.

'Mom, remember when I was little and I told you I flew to the zoo and met Elliot but his name was Mahshando?"

Stacy's eyes got big and she put her hand to her mouth. "Oh my goodness, I do. I was trying to remember that the other night after you were talking about *going* to the hospital."

"Back then you convinced me I had been dreaming. Then the other day when I went to the hospital I knew it wasn't a dream. Those first two times were kind of like accidents. I didn't think about doing it ahead of time, it just happened. But after the second time, I willed myself to go to the zoo and I taught Mahshando how to open the cages. Mtotah is the elephant at the end of the video. She called me a traveler and told me I look like Adrienne."

Then the doctor spoke again. "I knew Adrienne befriended an elephant when she was young, so I was wondering if it might be the same one. Were you in Estenson when they captured Mahshando?"

"Yes. I tried to get him to a high rocky ridge where they couldn't follow but they shot him with the dart before we could get there. Mom, that's when Amanda came and got me that morning. We went to her room and I took off."

At that moment Stacy believed, but Mike didn't.

"This is the biggest bunch of hooey nonsense I have ever heard!" he declared.

"Mr. Tenzio," Dr. Armitauge said. "When we started, I told you that we would be pushing your boundaries of belief to the edge. Please allow a small demonstration."

"Okay. Sure. I've got nothing better to do."

"Take this piece of paper and pen. Go out to your garage and write a short phrase on the paper. Then fold it, place it in your pocket, and return."

"Then?"

"Kita will be there and watch you write."

Mike shook his head in disbelief but he did take the paper and headed out to the garage.

When the back door closed, Kita leaned into her mom once again. Mike placed the paper on his workbench and wrote, *I found a treasure in San Antonio.* He folded the note twice and went back to the house. The three of them were waiting when he returned.

"She already told us what you wrote," Stacy said.

"What?"

"I found a treasure in San Antonio," Kita said.

Mike started chuckling. "This is some kind of elaborate trick. You guys have a camera out there focused on the bench, don't you? Is this one of your 'gotcha gags' honey? You hired this guy to come and play this part, didn't you? I have to give you credit, this is the best one yet. This is better than the surprise party last year at the Crompton's."

"Sorry Mike, but this is no trick of mine," Stacy said.

"Okay everybody, you can come out now," he shouted. "She got me." He walked to the next room looking for the others who he was convinced were in on the trick.

"There is no one else here, dear."

"Dad, am I really your treasure?"

"Yes, but this is still a trick."

"Let's try what I did with Amanda. She couldn't believe it at first either," Kita suggested.

"Why not? This is getting better all the time."

"Go anywhere outside you want. Then type on your phone three tricks you want Barney to do. When Barney finds you, hold your phone face up so I can see it. Then I'll tell Barney what to do."

"This ought to be good," Mike said.

After Barney laid on his back with his feet straight up, peed on the Bradley's fence, and pawed the ground at Mike's feet exactly five times, he became a believer too. He came back inside, slumped into his chair, shook his head, and trembled.

"I believe you, but I can't fit it into my mind."

Kita ran over and hugged him with all her strength.

Chapter 14
Evelyn and Ja'el

"Now that we all understand something of Kita's abilities I have to explain the gravity of the situation," said Dr. Armitauge.

"What do you mean?" Mike asked. "And by the way, how did you find her? How did you even know about her? You also said something about protecting her."

"I will try to answer all your questions, however, please understand that one evening will not be enough time to even begin to tell you all that is going on. First, Adrienne is Kita's biological grandmother. I was confident Kita existed but I didn't know her name, or where she was, or if she was an astral."

"What about her biological parents?" Stacy asked.

"I know absolutely nothing about her father. Adrienne doesn't either. Your biological mother's name was Dawn. She became estranged from Adrienne when she was in her late teens. Adrienne tried to keep track of her but she was out of the country when Dawn gave birth to Kita. Dawn was ill and died only weeks later. We only found out about that through hospital records. We have no idea of your father, where you were born, or how you came to be here."

"Kita was left at a church in San Antonio," Mike said.

"I see."

"What happened between Dawn and Adrienne?" asked Stacy.

"Please allow me to explain those details later. They are important but I should answer your other questions first. Astrals can communicate with animals so I am always on the look-out for stories that involve unusual animal activity. When I saw the video of the zoo escape, I started paying attention to Park City. I thought it might be Kita but I was not a hundred percent sure. When YouTube lit up with the dog video, I discovered Amanda."

"Dog video?" Stacy and Mike asked together.

Dr. Armitauge raised an eyebrow at Kita.

"I'll tell you about that later guys," she said.

"Anyway, the Free Elliot story was all over the news and there you were."

"But how did you get our address and —?"

"This is why it was imperative for me to come here."

Stacy stood up. "I have been rude. Doctor, can I get you something to drink?"

"Thank you Mrs. Tenzio. Water with no ice would be delightful."

"I think you better start calling me Stacy."

"Then please call me Arthur."

She returned moments later and handed a glass to Arthur.

He took a few sips and he began again. "There might be other people looking for you Kita; bad people."

"Are they the watchers?" Kita asked.

"You have heard of the watchers?" Arthur sounded surprised.

"Mtotah told me. She told me to be careful and that not all animals are good."

"A watcher is usually a dog. It has to be trained by an astral. They can alert their masters if an astral is near. There are accounts of humans who can see an astral but I have never known one."

"Other astrals?" Mike broke in. "There are more?"

Dr. Armitauge pulled a watch attached to a gold chain out of his vest pocket and looked at the time. "You are going to be wanting the full account I see."

"You know we are now," Mike answered.

"Very well, permit me to tell a story. It may take a while."

"We're not going anywhere," Mike said.

"I was born in Vouziers, a small village in northern France. When I was eleven years old the Germans invaded and my town became occupied territory. I joined the Resistance. Mostly, I carried messages. My father was a baker and I would do deliveries for him. Since he was forced to bake for the German soldiers, I had to deliver bread to them as well. They knew me and were never suspicious of me going to and fro. It was a perfect cover, carrying bread and messages at the same time. One night I was sent to a small farmhouse a couple of miles north of the village. When I arrived, I was told the message wasn't ready yet. Two men with rifles slung over their shoulders sat on either side of a small bed. A woman, who I thought was sleeping, was lying on the bed. Her hair was the purest gray I had ever seen. It was long and tied back. She was frail and I could see her veins through her skin. Just when I started to think she was dead, she opened her eyes and sat up. One of the men brought a bowl of stew to her. The other handed her a paper and a pen. She pushed his hand away with a gentle tap.

"Who is that?" she asked pointing at me.

"Messenger," the man with the soup answered.

"I have two messages," she said. "The first is for London and has to go now."

One of the men folded back a rug and opened a trap door in the floor under the table. He pulled out a radio transmitter. He cranked a handle on the side and handed the mouthpiece to the old woman.

"This is Ja'el."

There were three clicks in response.

"A stop and surround order has been given for Dunkirk. Acknowledge."

Three more clicks.

"They have orders to delay the attack."

Click, click, click. She handed the mic back and the man placed the radio back under the floor.

Then she looked at me. "Come here, boy." She waved her hand for me to approach.

"What is your name?"

"Arthur."

"Arthur, this is a message you must memorize and no one can hear it except Evelyn. Promise?"

"I promise."

"The message is: '*Come quickly. I'm dying. Ja'el.*'"

Both of the men bowed their heads.

"How will I know who she is?" I asked.

"If a woman comes to you and says she is Evelyn, you are to say, 'Grandmama.' She will answer by saying, 'travels lightly.'"

Mike Tenzio started pacing. "You mean to tell me that the Allies knew about Hitler's halt order at Dunkirk because of someone like Kita?"

Dr. Armitauge smiled. "I see you know your WWII history and you're following my story."

"What's Dunkirk?" Kita asked.

"It was an important event in WW II. The allies were in great danger but for some mysterious reason the Germans delayed their attack and most of the allies were able to get away." her dad answered. "Please continue, Doctor."

"When I returned to my commander, I told him I had a message for someone named Evelyn and that I had to deliver it personally. He told me to go home and wait. Two days later a young woman entered the bakery. Her peasant clothing, plain hairstyle, and tattered scarf could barely conceal her extraordinary beauty.

"I am looking for Arthur," she said.

"That is me."

"I am Evelyn."

"Grandmama."

"Travels lightly," she said.

I walked to her side of the counter.

"You have a message for me?" she asked.

"Yes."

"Tell me please."

"Come quickly. I am dying. Ja'el."

When I finished speaking, her body crumpled a bit and her eyes started to water.

"Do you know where she is?" she asked.

"Yes."

"Take me there."

I grabbed two baskets and put loaves in each. I handed one to her. She looked at me with questioning eyes.

"We pretend we're delivering," I explained.

When we entered the farmhouse, Ja'el was sitting on the side of her bed. Evelyn ran over, sat down next to her, and they hugged.

"Grandmama you can't go. I need you." She was sobbing and burying her face in the old woman's shoulder.

"You must carry on. I know you can."

"What about the book?"

Ja'el put her mouth to Evelyn's ear and whispered. Then she removed a ring from one of her fingers and slipped it into Evelyn's hand.

A third man I had never seen before came into the house.

"Germans are coming! They're minutes away!"

One of the other men opened the trap door and pushed Evelyn and me down the opening that led to a space under the house. He followed.

"What about Grandmama?" Evelyn protested.

"Go, child!" Ja'el urged.

The man tipped a large wooden barrel on its side and motioned for us to hurry. Under the barrel was a hole leading to a tunnel.

"It comes out in the barn," he said.

We dropped through and he rolled the barrel back in place. We crawled in total darkness. I felt our way with my hands. The walls and ceiling were lined with boards but the floor was cool dirt. There was gunfire and shouting, then more gunfire. We crawled faster and kept going until the tunnel ended at a crude ladder. We sat still and listened. The gunfire stopped but there was still some shouting. I went up the ladder and pushed open a door on the floor of the barn just enough to see. None of the soldiers were in the barn. We climbed out, went up to the hayloft, and peeked out between slats in the barn wall. A German soldier walked out of the house. He was holding the radio transmitter and smiling. Then another soldier came out. He was carrying Ja'el over his shoulder like a sack of flour. He put her in the back seat of the officer's car. Evelyn gasped. Then she fell next to me like she had passed out. A few seconds later she was back to life.

"She's dead," she said.

"How do you know?" I asked.

"It is something I will have to tell you later, maybe. Her three guards are dead also."

At this point, the doctor took a break and sipped some water.

"This is where you got involved, isn't it," Stacy said.

Dr. Armitauge nodded.

"We waited until they drove off, then made our way back to town.

As you may have guessed, Evelyn took over for Ja'el. She had always been afraid of traveling and didn't like the toll it took on her body."

"Is that why I feel really tired when I get back in my body?" Kita asked.

"Yes, there is an effect. It is something you and I will have to talk about."

"Okay," Kita said.

"As I was saying, Evelyn never wanted to use her powers, but she hated Hitler. There was one problem, however, she had a seven-year-old daughter named Marie. Our family took Marie in and watched over her like she was one of our own while Evelyn went to work for the Allies. It was Evelyn who told the code breakers at Bletchley Park that a German weather boat carrying an Enigma machine was in the North Sea. She was also responsible for getting the date that the Germans were going to launch their air attack for *Adler tag*. That information saved the RAF."

"What's the RAF?" Kita asked.

"The Brit's Royal Air Force," Mike answered.

Arthur continued. "Evelyn's last piece of information was the location of Hitler's final bunker. When the war ended she took Marie to America. She learned how to use her special skills to make large sums of money. She used that money to pay for my brother and me to come to America. She sent us to Medical School and picked me to be her sentinel."

"What's a sentinel?" asked Kita.

"It is a guard, and a protector, and a keeper of the history. I hope to tell you about all of these things another time. Marie grew to be a beautiful woman and had a soft spot in her heart for my brother. They were married and had a baby girl. They named her Adrienne."

Kita jumped up. "Does that mean we're related?"

"In a way it does. Francis is your great-grandfather and I am his brother."

"Is he still alive?"

"He is."

"Will I meet him too?"

"All in good time I hope."

Kita sat back down but now she was leaning forward on the edge of the sofa and tapping her foot.

Arthur continued, "When Adrienne was nineteen, Evelyn took on an especially dangerous mission for the CIA in a battle against drug lords in Mexico. Before she left, she gave Adrienne the ring that had been passed to her by Ja'el. She said she 'had a feeling.'"

"Is that the ring I wore tonight?"

"Yes. She also taught her about the Book of Ciphers."

"The book Evelyn asked about earlier?" Mike asked.

"Yes. There has always been one astral on earth, sometimes two, but there has never been more than three at the same time. Not all astrals have been good. The Book of Ciphers is a book of astral history. More importantly, it contains knowledge of how astrals can expand their powers. Fortunately, it has never been in the hands of an evil astral. It contains all the secrets of the astrals and many human secrets that should remain that way. You think the earth has troubles now. It would be catastrophic if that book landed in the wrong hands. Anyway, Evelyn never returned from Mexico. It was a plane crash that we're not sure was an accident. And now we think Adrienne is being held captive somewhere in Australia, and Kita, here you are."

"Wait a minute," Mike broke in. "You're not going to involve my daughter in some kind of invisible worldwide conflict."

"I am here to keep her out of one. So these next few moments are important. Kita, how many times have you traveled since you went to the hospital?"

"Just around the house or anywhere?"

"Out in public," Arthur answered.

"There was the zoo, then Estenson, and then the dogs. Three."

"How was your trip to Estenson?"

"Amanda pointed me in the right direction. I flew pretty slow until I got to the water tower. Then it was instant."

"How slow is slow?" Arthur asked.

"It took me more than five minutes to get there."

"Five minutes," Mike exclaimed. "That's over forty miles away."

"I came back even faster."

"We know there is an astral on earth now, who is bent toward evil. We do not know who he is or where he is. We don't know if he and the people he works with know about you but we must act as if they are looking for you. He won't find you as long as you don't travel. I won't leave here without you giving me your word you will stay put. If by some chance he is here when you travel, he could find you. Do I have your promise?"

"Yes."

"Why couldn't he find her the same way you did?" Mike asked.

"I am confident no one knows about the space distortion as I do. My background in quantum physics and electro-magnetics is quite rare. I am sure no one has developed a detecting software as I have. The zoo video will never be seen. We erased the zoo's copy on their own system. I now own the only copy. However, he might realize unusual animal activity is something to keep an eye out for. The dog video has gone viral. We must be careful."

"Can we see it?"

Dr. Armitauge clicked another icon and Barney and friends were in action. Mike recognized the Stenburg's Rottweiler. "Wow," was all he said.

"Why would this person be looking for Kita?" Stacy asked.

"To bend her and if he can't do that, to imprison her, or worse."

All three Tenzios eyes widened. Stacy pulled Kita in close.

"And if he knows anything about the book at all, and hopefully he doesn't, he will want it at all costs."

"What do you mean by bend?" asked Mike.

"All astrals are born with what I call a bent. Some are bent toward love, honor, compassion, and justice. Others are bent toward extortion, violence, power, and wealth. However, there is a history of astrals going against their original bent. This has been rare and every case came to a horrible end."

"Why?"

"Because an astral with a bad bent has never been turned to the good. It has only been the other way around."

"You are telling us some guy with superpowers is out to either turn my Kita into some kind of monster or kill her and our only hope of that not happening, is you?"

"I'm sorry but that is the proper assessment. I have come to make a proposal."

"What kind of proposal?" Kita asked.

"There are two ways we can move forward. First, there have always been astrals throughout time who have chosen to never live the astral life. They seldom or never traveled and kept their ability a secret. They didn't like the toll traveling took on their body so they chose to not travel."

"What is this toll on the body?" Stacy asked.

"Traveling increases the aging rate. When a traveler is young, it is barely noticeable. If the distances are short the effects are minimal. But the older a traveler gets the more serious the effect. Long distances take even a heavier toll. It is something you will have to consider. Evelyn was completely gray and had osteoporosis before she was forty."

Kita didn't like the sound of that.

"We also know there have even been astrals who never found out about their abilities. You could act like one of those. You can decide to never travel, never communicate with animals again, and never tell a soul. If you choose this path, it is probable you will be safe. The other path is to come with me. I can train and teach you the ways of an astral. I can help you discover your other abilities, strengthen the ones you already have, and show you how to protect yourself. If you choose this path, there will be no turning back."

"Where would I do this training?" asked Kita.

"I own a private island on Lake Superior. If you and Amanda would agree to come and visit me, we can begin your training, and I can protect you."

"Why Amanda?"

"She is in the video. If they can't get to you, they could try to capture her and use her to lure you out. Plus, I have some things I must teach her also."

"Is this the special school Adrienne told Mtotah about?"

"Yes."

"Do I have to decide tonight?"

"If you don't come with me tonight, in a way, you have made a decision."

"I need to know one more thing," Kita said.

"Of course. Anything," the doctor answered.

"Am I human?"

"Kita!" Stacy protested.

"That is quite all right," Arthur said. "It's actually an astute question. I like to say astrals are human and a little bit more."

"I'm not an alien or from another dimension or something?"

"You are not an alien," Dr. Armitauge answered.

"We need time to think about this," Mike said. "If I understand you right, you're talking about changing her life forever."

"You have grasped the situation correctly."

"As I said, we need some time."

"All right then, I won't force you. I do have a man who will be keeping an eye on the girls just in case. He will be discreet. You will never know he's about. Although he is highly trained and committed, I can make no promise."

"As you said, these people would not only have to see the dog video, they'd have to know what they're looking for. That should give us some time." It was Mike's final statement on the matter.

"I did say something about the Elliot campaign when I came. I'm sure I can convince the zoo to send Mahshando to that preserve in Arizona."

"Really!?" exclaimed Kita.

"Oh, I'm quite sure."

"Maybe that's enough for one night," said Stacy. "I don't think I can take in any more."

"I will take my leave then. And Kita, stay away from camera interviews. Promise me, no traveling."

"I promise."

* * *

In bed that night Kita was imagining Ja'el and the Nazi soldiers, the gray hair, and the skin that Arthur could see through. She wondered who the bad people were that were after her and what she would do if she met the other traveler. Restless visions of Mahshando wandering free in the preserve, a real grandmother out there somewhere who looked like her, training on a secret island, and the feeling of power that surged through her when she wore the ring, kept sleep beyond her reach. What really prevented her mind from rest, however, was the decision. She didn't know if she could give up talking with animals. She wanted to learn more about who she was, yet she was more afraid then she had ever been in her life. Maybe a quiet, normal life would be just fine. Then again, maybe because of what she had the dogs do to Longstreet at lunch, that wasn't possible now. She wrestled with all these thoughts long after the spring peepers had shut down for the night.

Chapter 15

Compelling Video

"Come and look at this," Bayne said.

Colton Wrancor sauntered over to Bayne's desk and peered over his shoulder. Bayne played the video through twice."

"Well?"

"It's the girl with the copper hair," Colton said. "She's the only one with no reaction."

"What about the dogs?"

"There's precision, cooperation, and they took off as soon as the cigarettes flew out of the backpack. They were being directed."

"By the girl?" asked Bayne.

"Can't be the girl. We can see her and she's fully awake."

"But she acts like she knows something."

"Maybe. Where is this anyway?" Wrancor asked.

"It's at a middle school in Alkorn Heights, a suburb of Park City, in Minnesota."

"America?"

"Impressed to see you're up on your geography. I want you to go and check this girl out. I want to know her name, where she lives, friends, everything."

"You mean travel?"

"Yes."

"I've never gone that far before. Look at what happened to me when I went to Brisbane. I had to sleep for a whole day when I got back. And it weakened me. I'd be totally wiped out going all the way to America. Fly me over in the jet."

"You can do it. Remember, you didn't even know you were tired until you got back. You can rest then. I need information now. Two days from now might be too late."

"I don't like it."

"I telling you to go, so you will go!" Bayne commanded.

"You've been doing a lot of demanding lately, Claude."

"You work for me, Colton. Don't forget that. And you know better than to call me Claude."

"Oh, I haven't forgotten who I work for," Wrancor answered. He picked up a silver pen from Bayne's desk and gave it a twirl. "I was just wondering how I'd do as an independent contractor."

Bayne leaned back in his chair and clasped his hands behind his head. "You could always try. But you should consider the consequences others have experienced who decided they no longer wanted to be loyal to me."

"Threats Claude? I'm the goose that lays the golden eggs."

"You're not the only one anymore. I have the woman."

"Seems like she isn't going to be too cooperative."

"You know I have my ways," Bayne said.

"Let me get a little rest first. I was out pretty late last night."

"I've told you before, your lifestyle is going to ruin you."

"My lifestyle is the only reason I keep doing this stuff and you know it."

"Four hours, then you go!" Bayne stood and pointed east.

"Okay." Wrancor went to his back room without answering and set the alarm on his phone.

* * *

Oliver Brandt used his professionally crafted counterfeit press credentials to get an audience with Connie Smythe at Capitol Zoo. On her part, she was quite thrilled to be meeting with a top journalist from Animal Universe Magazine. As was her habit, she was too lazy to check if Gordon Cutherton was on staff or even if he ever produced anything for the publication.

"Please come in Mr. Cutherton. What can I do for you today?" She pointed to one of the chairs in front of her desk. The only window in her office looked out over the seal exhibit. Four pens were strewn amongst papers piled all over her desk. Some of the books on her bookshelf were upside down, some were laying flat, and others didn't even have the spines facing out. Her coat tree overflowed with coats on top of jackets on top of shirts.

"I'm doing a piece on the top ten zoos in North America," Oliver began. "I was going to include Capitol Zoo in my article until this business with the gorilla became front-page news."

"We have that all under control now. I'm sure that won't lower our standing. Especially since the press saw our humane manner of recapturing him," she answered.

"What about this campaign these two middle school girls are running. I see they have reached $12,000.00 and are climbing. Is it true you have refused to meet with them?"

"Why meet with them? Wouldn't want to get their hopes up. We have no plans on selling Elliot. He is one of our main attractions and more so now that he has been in the news."

"Very well then, would you mind looking at a video I came across recently. I think you'll find it fascinating."

"I'd love too," she cooed.

Oliver set his iPad on her desk and clicked on the folder marked

PCZ. It only took a few seconds before Connie Smythe's eyes bugged out and her hands started shaking. She was watching the video of the zoo escape in its entirety.

"Where did you get this?" she demanded.

"I think that's irrelevant at this point," Oliver answered. "However, I am assuming your concoction about animal extremists hacking your system has something to do with the fact you're not interested in the public finding out what really happened. Am I right?"

"Go on."

"I can make sure it stays a secret."

"Is this blackmail or something?"

"Not exactly, but close. Meet with the girls, set a fair price for the gorilla, and let them win. It will be good publicity for you and people will still be willing to come to a zoo where they can naively believe the animals are happy. Plus, you won't have to explain to your board of directors or the public why you made up an elaborate story about animal activists and kept the real story to yourself."

"If I don't?"

Oliver smiled. "You will. Just think how good that story would look in my magazine. I can see the byline: Zoo Administrator Helps Girls Love On Animals."

Connie Smythe contemplated that idea for more than a few seconds. "You aren't really connected to the magazine, are you." she said.

"Free lance. I'm sure they would love a story about what really happened at your zoo."

"I will have to talk with others about this," she said.

"Oh and one more thing," Oliver said. "The girls might want to free the female elephant too."

Chapter 16
48K

Getting on the bus that morning, Kita was all set to tell Amanda about the visit from Dr. Armitauge until she spotted a crude poster taped to their usual seat. It was an enlarged photo of two gorillas with a picture of Kita's head cut out and pasted on one of the apes and Amanda's on the other. The caption read: Help Send the Gorillas to Arizona.

Amanda held Kita back.

"You are going to have to claw his eyes out another day," she whispered.

Amanda removed the poster, folded it with a crisp crease, and gingerly slipped it into her backpack. Then she looked at Longstreet and Wartworth and pointed at the overhead video camera in the front of the bus.

"You really are stupid Longstream," she said.

His smirk vanished when her intent finally passed through the immense thickness firmly cemented between his skin and his brain.

"You and the principal must know each other pretty well by now," Amanda said.

* * *

Wrancor was hovering next to one of the picnic tables outside the school waiting for the girl with the copper hair. Although he was an expert traveler and had memorized the Google maps screen before he left, it took ten minutes of buzzing around Alkorn Heights before he found the school. When Amanda and Kita got off bus 317, Wrancor smiled to himself. It was a snide, wicked smile. He followed the girls into the school and watched them set up their table in front of a poster of a giant red thermometer. It was displaying the fundraising progress to free some gorilla. It was up to $19,000.00. Kids stopped by the table to contribute and take a sticker.

Connie Smythe approached their table. She was wearing her official zoo uniform with her gold colored nametag displayed above the flap of her left pocket.

"I was wondering if I could have a few words with you girls?"

"Sure," they said together.

"My name is Connie Smythe. I am the director of Capitol Zoo."

"We know," Amanda said. "We've been trying to get a hold of you for a few days now."

'Well, yes. Sorry about that. Anyway, I think we should be able to negotiate a reasonable price for Elliot so he can go to that zoo in Arizona."

"It's the Aegis Preserve," Kita snapped back. "It's not a zoo. People there aren't allowed to stare at the animals and they're not in cages."

"Oh yes. The Aegis Preserve."

"We're listening," said Amanda.

"How much have you raised so far?"

Amanda pointed to the progress poster on the wall behind her.

"Well on the way," Smythe said. "I have been authorized to allow Elliot to be moved for a reimbursement to the zoo of forty-eight thousand dollars."

"We can make that happen," said Amanda. "But you'll need to sign this." She reached in her backpack and pulled out a hard sided folder. Inside the folder was a contract that Amanda had created on her computer. It explained the who, what, and where. It had blanks for amounts, dates, and signatures.

Connie Smythe read it through. "Did you prepare this yourself?"

"Yes."

"Very impressive."

All three signed after Amanda wrote in the amount. Then they shook on it.

"You are amazing," Kita told Amanda after Connie Smythe left.

"Not really. You can find almost anything online."

* * *

Wrancor followed the girls around school for their first few classes. He had never been around so many adolescents at the same time. They were driving him crazy. *This place is actually the zoo*, he thought to himself. Then he had an idea; a devious, brilliant idea. I should go to the real zoo and see that gorilla they're talking about. I can come back here later.

It took him less than five minutes to find the zoo. Elliot backed away when Wrancor entered the glass enclosure.

"Hey there big fella."

Elliot stepped backed another two feet.

"No need to be afraid. You've seen someone like me before, haven't you?"

"I have."

"Then what's the problem?"

"She's not black like you."

Wrancor looked at the greenish hue of his traveler's body. "What are you talking about? I'm not black. I'm green."

"Your heart is black."

"What do you mean black?"

"Her heart has light, yours *is* darkness."

Colton was taken aback. Most of his transactions with animals involved training them, using them, or avoiding them. He had never thought of an animal commenting on his personality. To be described as black hearted and full of darkness by a strange gorilla startled him.

"What's her name, this other visitor?"

Before Wrancor had a chance to react, Mahshando was on him. He grabbed him around the throat and threw him through the glass wall and halfway down the eastern pathway.

"Never come here again!" He roared, beating his chest.

Wrancor picked himself up and went back to the cage, making sure he didn't go inside the glass.

"A bit protective, I see. If I have my way, you will never see the outside of this glass house as long as you live."

Elliot turned his back to the ugly visitor.

* * *

After school, the girls were back at their table. Amanda opened her laptop to check on their GoFundMe status.

"Wow! Look at this!" she said. "Somebody just made a $30,000.00 donation!"

A number of others around the table heard the news and started clapping. Some even hugged each other. Amanda took a magnum sized red marker and filled in the thermometer. She drew spray marks pouring out over the $48,000.00 line. The girls packed up their table and went to tell Mr. Rister.

* * *

It was one of those perfect days in Minnesota that only happens in May. Blue sky, gentle southern breeze, and lilac scent lingering in the air. The girls walked home.

Oliver Brandt followed at a safe distance.

Colton Wrancor was hovering two feet off their heels.

"I think I know who made the big donation," said Kita.

"You do?"

Kita blurted out what she had been holding in all day, every detail of Dr. Armitauge's visit, the history, the book, the island, Adrienne, everything. Little did she know an invisible stalker heard every word she said.

"This is incredibly crazy. Did you ask him about the generational thing?"

"What do you mean?"

"You know, in the story. Ja'el, then Evelyn, then Adrienne, and then you. It skips a generation, Grandma/granddaughter repeats itself."

"I didn't think about that."

"What's this doctor guy like?"

"He is really old and he is like a genius or something, but he's nice."

"Have you decided what you're going to do?"

"I don't know what to do."

"You have to go with him," Amanda urged. "What would have happened if Wonder Woman just sat around on Paradise Island?"

"I know."

"What about your parents?"

"We haven't talked about it yet. They were totally freaked out last night."

"I'll bet they were."

The girls stopped at the end of their driveways.

"Come over tonight after you talk to your parents," said Amanda.

"I will."

Colton Wrancor sped off to Melbourne.

Oliver Brandt watched the girls go inside their houses and felt secure about their safety. It was most unfortunate he didn't have his dog, Ranger with him, a well-trained watcher.

Chapter 17
Bayne

When Colton returned from Park City Bayne was leafing through a new brochure displaying a sixty-five foot Sea Ray L Class and jotting down a list of options he thought should be added to have the perfect cruiser.

"Well?"

Colton handed Bayne a slip of paper with the girl's names and addresses. Then he plopped down on the sofa.

"I need to sleep and I need to eat something. I feel like I just wandered through the outback for a week without food or water."

"Information first," insisted Bayne.

"The Griffith girl is just a friend. The Tenzio girl is the traveler. Some old guy named Armitauge knows about her and wants to train her. He has a compound on some island in Lake Superior and I think our captive is the girl's grandmother. Her real name is Adrienne."

Bayne smiled. "You've done well."

"Oh, and one more thing. There *is* a book."

Bayne jumped to his feet. "I knew it!"

He reached for his phone. "I want the plane ready in one hour," he said. "There will be five passengers and a dog."

"Where to?" the voice on the other end asked.

"Park City, Minnesota in the U.S."

"Am I one of the five?" Colton asked.

"Obviously. Get those girls and bring them back!"

"What about my sleep? That distance wiped me out and I feel weak."

"You can sleep on the plane."

"Very well." Wrancor dragged himself to the kitchen and looked in the refrigerator. "How come you never have any food in here?"

"Lay down for a few minutes. I'll call something up for you. What do you want?"

"Big breakfast."

Bayne opened his phone. "I want a one inch thick ham steak and four eggs with fried potatoes, plenty of juice, and some pastries. Bring a bowl of fruit with some cream too."

Colton laid back down on the sofa. He decided to keep a few secrets to himself. He didn't tell Bayne there were at the most three astrals on earth at any one time or that you needed a ring to read the book. He didn't mention Elliot's pronouncement of him having a black heart and he remained silent about the fact that others knew Bayne's captive was in trouble.

Bayne walked over to the sofa and handed the Sea Ray brochure to Wrancor. "Bring the girl back and this is yours."

* * *

Claude Bayne had been an only child and never knew his father. His mother was a waitress in a back street pub in Canberra. She wasn't all that interested in mothering and didn't so much raise him as let him hang around. Fending for himself became a way of life. He did small chores for the owner of the bar and all the regulars knew him by name. By the time he was ten, he was making *special* deliveries for one of those regulars, a man named Vincent Newsome. Bayne never peeked inside the small packages he carried but by the looks of the people who received them, he had his ideas. He squirreled away almost every dollar he earned. He did, however, buy himself a bike and a small backpack. Then he asked for more assignments. When he was twelve he was attacked by a group of older boys intent on stealing his pack. He fought back but they slashed the straps of his bag and took it. One of the boys carved a long gash on the side of his neck with a knife. A second boy smashed out the spokes of his bike with a metal bar, while a third boy stomped on his knee.

"That's for fighting back," they said.

Although the cut on his neck ran from his ear to his shoulder and spewed out a lot of blood, it was not fatal. He made it back to the pub and Mr. Newsome called a doctor in to stitch him up.

What those boys didn't know was that Claude Bayne was street smart beyond his years. His backpack carried a fake package of baking soda. The real packages he kept tightly wrapped to his waist with a custom sash of his own creation. When he showed Vincent Newsome that he still had the goods, he was rewarded with two one-hundred-dollar bills. He bought another backpack, fixed his bike, and continued his runs.

On his first day back in business, the same boys stopped him again. Bayne handed his backpack over.

"Think you're funny? We want the real stuff."

Suddenly a van screeched to a halt three feet from the scene. Doors flung open and men jumped out carrying hoods and guns. In seconds, two of the boys were subdued and shoved into the van. The men kept the smallest one out on the sidewalk. He was kicking and squirming.

"Take a good look at this bloke." One of the gunmen grabbed his captive by the hair and turned his head forcing him to look at Bayne. "Go tell your other friends this lad has protection. Understand?"

The boy nodded. He looked in the van at his partners who now had hoods over their heads.

"What about —?"

"Count yourself lucky we need a messenger."

Bayne saw the third boy around town a few times after that but he never again saw the two who were carried away in the van.

By the time he was sixteen, he occasionally drove Mr. Newsome to specific destinations. He never asked why and always remained in the car when Newsome went into a building. When he reached twenty, Bayne was Newsome's most trusted personal assistant. During these formative years, Bayne learned that loyalty and the ability to keep a secret meant promotion. Wealth meant power and power meant other people carried out your orders. Power also meant you could use fear as an intense motivator. Power meant enemies could be done away with. These were lessons he never forgot.

Then things changed. Newsome quit running drugs and moved his entire operation to Melbourne. He bought a former sheep station north of the city and turned it into an estate, complete with horses, exotic animals, a swimming pool bigger than the old pub in Canberra, an airstrip, and a security force. A frail, older gentleman occupied one wing of the house. Bayne was never invited to any of the meetings between this new man and Newsome. He did not like not being in the know but he did what he was told. His job now was to pick up an occasional briefcase from a businessman or a politician, be Mr. Newsome's exclusive driver, monitor the security system, and the people who ran it. This went on for several years.

Vincent Newsome called Bayne into his office one day. The outcome of that meeting vaulted Claude Bayne into a whole new realm of existence.

"My guest from the north wing has died. I want you to arrange for his cremation and I want it to be discreet. Use our friends on

Boundary Road." Then he handed Bayne a small briefcase along with a card. The address on the card was handwritten. "When you're done taking care of the cremation I want you to go to this address in Geelong. A woman will meet you there. You are to give her this briefcase and bring back a young boy named Colton."

* * *

Adrienne was sitting on the veranda when Bayne arrived for his second visit with her.

"I see you have decided to enjoy the view." He walked onto the veranda and sat on the other side of a small round table. Cerberus was faithfully at his side, alert as always.

Adrienne didn't answer.

"I have some new information that should add some clarity to our discussion."

A young woman wearing khaki pants and a blue shirt came out the front door and stood to Bayne's side. "Can I get you anything, sir?"

"I'll have coffee and a scone. Do you want anything?" He looked toward Adrienne.

"Just coffee," she said.

He waited until their coffee was delivered before he continued. "You see, Ms. Harcourt, or should I say, *Adrienne*. We've found your granddaughter. In fact, this very minute my associates are picking her up and bringing her here. I don't think your friend, what's his name, Armitauge, will be able to protect her."

Adrienne willed herself to stay calm. One skill she had developed was being able to go astral yet remain in her physical body. This allowed her to see the astral world without being noticed herself. It was the trick she did to get the wallabies to look in her pocket the day Wrancor discovered her. She sipped her coffee as slow as possible and scanned all around to see if Colton Wrancor was about. All was clear. During her time in captivity she had played out numerous scenarios, none of them involved the girl being captured.

She knew pretending time was over.

"If you know my name and you know about the doctor and that I have a granddaughter, you've learned quite a bit."

"Oh yes and that book I mentioned the other day, the one you pretended to know nothing about. I know it exists."

How in the world did he find out about all this? she thought to herself. *Maybe the lure of the book might keep me alive. I'll tell him a little and see what happens.*

"It's called the Book of Ciphers."

"And?"

"It contains the history of the travelers. Supposedly, it also has instructions on how to expand our powers."

By the look on Bayne's face, Adrienne knew that bit of information had its intended effect.

"What do you mean supposedly?"

"I have tried —"

"You will bring me that book," Bayne interrupted.

"I will?"

"Oh yes. If not, I will inflict immeasurable pain on your granddaughter while you watch. I am a man who gets the things he wants and when I don't, I tend to be rather unpleasant."

"There is just a slight problem with your plan."

"You think so?"

"Like I was trying to say before. The book is in an ancient language that no longer exists. Even though I have seen it, I have not been able to read it. Believe me, I've tried. Maybe there is someone who can but I don't know who that is."

"You're lying. You will bring me the book. You will read it or the girl will meet with agony of immeasurable proportions."

"How do you expect me to bring you the book? Are you going to let me go pick it up?"

"Oh, I think I might be able to arrange for it to be delivered."

Adrienne didn't like the sound of that. She was also worried that somehow her S.O.S. message hadn't gotten through. She hoped Arthur had sent someone but she had been out looking three different nights and there was no sign of help. Or, if Bayne's tech guy was somewhere besides Melbourne when he tried opening the phone, those coordinates would have been sent instead. Things were getting worse and she wasn't happy with any of the scenarios playing out in her mind.

This Bayne must not be allowed to have the upper hand.

Chapter 18
The Walk Home

Bayne's private Gulfstream arrived in Park City in less than seventeen hours. Bauman Field, a small airport on the south side of the city, specialized in private jet traffic. They also provided a service arranging the rental of vehicles with unique characteristics. A top of the line Range Rover modified with bulletproof glass, and airless, solid rubber tires, was waiting for Wrancor and his companions at touchdown. They landed at one in the afternoon. There was plenty of time to reach Alkorn Heights Middle School before the dismissal bell. They parked on the street across from the school parking lot.

Oliver Brandt was parked two blocks up the street, keeping his eyes on Kita and Amanda's usual walking route home. He became a bit more alert when he saw them strolling down the sidewalk. Before he could react, the Range Rover pulled up next to the girls. The side doors swung open. Wrancor and three others jumped out. Brandt leaped out of his car and sprinted full bore down the street. When he got to the sidewalk side of the Rover, Wrancor had already dragged Kita inside. Two more men were trying to wrestle Amanda into the SUV. She was kicking at them with wild fury, but only hitting air. However, one of the men crumpled to the ground from a fierce smash to the back of his neck before the other one even knew Oliver Brandt was on them. The second man turned just in time to receive a violent blow to the throat from Oliver's heel. A third man pulled a gun. He was too slow. He went to his knees in writhing pain. Oliver broke his wrist when he disarmed him. A precise knee to his face put him out of his misery.

"Run Amanda!" Oliver shouted.

She ran and hid on the backside of a giant elm. Wrancor rolled down a side window and fired at Brandt. Kita pushed him in the back, throwing off his aim. He knocked her down with a smash to the jaw with the butt of his gun. Oliver rolled to the ground, pulled his weapon from the back of his waistband, and fired back.

Wrancor took one in the shoulder.

"Go, go, go!" Wrancor shouted.

Napier, the driver, stomped on the gas, and the Rover took off down the street.

Oliver emptied his gun into the rear tires to no avail. Then he grabbed the gun off the man he disarmed and fired at the back window. The bullets bounced off and the SUV sped out of range. He searched the bodies of all three downed men. He collected phones, guns, ammo, and two knives. There were no wallets. No IDs.

The action was over in less than thirty seconds.

He went to fetch Amanda. She was on her knees, shaking.

"We have to go Amanda."

She looked up at him. Her face was a mess of tears. "I thought you were the man from the magazine."

"I am. Dr. Armitauge assigned me to guard you and Kita."

"But they took Kita."

"I can't do anything about that now. I have to get *you* to safety."

She looked at the three men laying on the ground. She looked back at Oliver. "Are they dead?"

"No, but they'll be out for a while and they will be feeling none too pleasant when they come to. We have to leave now! We can't be here when the police get here. Come on." He started running to his car. He pulled her along by the wrist as gently as he could.

He drove four blocks, took a left, and drove a half-mile to a mini-mall. The parking lot was almost full but he found a place to back in.

Then he took out his phone and called Dr. Armitauge.

"They have her," Oliver said.

"How?"

"Five of them in a bulletproof SUV. They already had Kita inside by the time I got there. I took out three of them and shot the fourth one in the shoulder."

"What about Amanda?"

"She's with me."

"Take her home. Make her promise to say nothing. Pick me up at the Crystal Airport. I should be there in less than two hours."

"What about Kita's parents?"

"I will contact them."

Oliver drove Amanda straight home. He walked over to her side of the car and opened the door for her.

"You're safe for now, Amanda," he said.

"What about Kita?"

"We're going to work on getting her back. But I need you to promise me, not a word to anyone about this. You are going to have to pretend nothing has happened. Can you do that?"

"What about Stacy and Mike?"

"We will contact them. I am going to pick up Dr. Armitauge. We will be back here tonight. Promise me you'll say nothing?"

"I'll try.

* * *

Wrancor's clothes stuck to the wound on his shoulder and slowed the bleeding. He called Bayne.

"What's the status?"

"We have her but we have casualties. Some guy came out of nowhere and attacked us. He took out Carson and Wirtz before we even knew he was there. He knows some advanced martial arts. Everything went so fast it was a blur. He got Holmes too."

"Are they dead?"

"Not sure."

"What about the other girl?"

"She got away."

"We have the prize and that's all we need. Don't bother going after the other one."

"I have a bullet in my shoulder," Wrancor complained.

"How bad?"

"The bleeding has stopped but it hurts like hell."

"Are you faint?"

"No."

"Take some painkillers and you'll be okay until you get here. I'll have a doctor waiting."

* * *

When the police arrived at 310 Craft Street, a small crowd had gathered in front of the house of an elderly widow named Ginny Stohler. Some were students who had been walking home. Others were curious neighbors who had heard the gunshots. They all were staring at the three men laying on her lawn, still out cold. Mrs. Stohler was the one who called the police when she heard the gunfire.

"What exactly did you see ma'am?" asked the young officer.

"I saw a white SUV screeching away and a man was shooting at it. Then he took guns from these men and ran away with a copper headed girl. They drove off in a green car."

"Is that all ma'am?"

"There might be one more thing but I'm not sure. It all happened so fast. I think there was a young girl in the SUV and one of the men hit her in the face."

Chapter 19
Neighbors

When Kita regained consciousness the plane was well on its way to the West Coast. Wrancor sat across from her, slumped back, and sleeping. The bloodstain that covered the upper right half of his shirt had dried to a crust. Kita looked out the window at the ground below. Little brown and green squares outlined by skinny roads spread out everywhere. Farther away, a black river meandered off into the distance. Her hands were strapped down snug to the arms of her chair. She pulled and pulled. All she got for her struggle was sore wrists.

She stretched her leg forward and nudged Wrancor's knee with her toe.

He opened his eyes. "What do you want?"

"I have to use the bathroom."

"Hold it."

"I can't."

"All right, but if you hit me or kick me again, I will tie you, gag you, and put a bag over your head. We have over fifteen hours yet to go, so make up your mind."

"Fifteen hours, where are we going?"

"You'll find out when you get there."

"I won't hit you," Kita said. "Besides, it doesn't look like I have anywhere to go anyway."

Wrancor released her straps. The bathroom was in the back of the plane. Once inside, she left her body and came back out into the cabin to have a look around.

She froze.

Wrancor was hovering in the aisle, waiting for her. His astral body looked like it was covered with alligator skin that was the darkest of greens. His fingernails were long curved claws and his eyes were a fierce orange with black pupils no bigger than pinholes.

"Going somewhere?" he asked.

* * *

Molly Griffith raced from the car through the back door and into the kitchen. "Amanda! Amanda! Are you here?"

"Right here, Mom. What's going on?" Amanda called back.

"I just heard on the radio about a shooting near your school. The police are looking for a girl with copper hair who was dragged off with one of the shooters."

"Wow."

"I don't know too many girls with copper hair, do you?"

"No. Maybe it was a redhead or something. They actually said copper?"

Molly studied her daughter's face. "Is there something you're not telling me?"

Amanda hesitated.

"What is it?" Molly urged.

"There is something but I have to wait and *tell* you after Kita's parents come over.

"Mike and Stacy are coming over?"

"Yes."

"Why? Has something happened to Kita?"

Amanda started sobbing and ran into her mother's arms.

* * *

One of the guards knocked on the door of Adrienne's room.

"Yes?"

"Mr. Bayne wants another word with you."

Adrienne followed the man across the yard to a six stall garage. They stopped outside and stood on the concrete apron. Bayne was leaning against a black Mercedes puffing on a cigar and talking to someone wearing a mechanic's coveralls. He came out when he saw her and motioned for the guard to leave them alone.

"I thought you'd like to know there may be a family reunion soon."

"How so?"

"We have the girl."

Adrienne held her face expressionless.

"A friend of yours tried to stop us. He took out three of my men in seconds so I think we can stop pretending that you're not in the big leagues. Just so you know, any attempt to come in here and rescue you will be met with extreme force. Believe me, I have it."

"I don't have a friend who 'takes out' people. And as far as a rescue, how would anyone know where to look for me?"

"How indeed."

* * *

Amanda stopped crying but her eyes were puffy and her nose still red when Carter Griffith came home from work. Six foot six, thin as a rail, and a shiny baldhead made him easy to spot when he strode across the campus at Hamline University where he taught business ethics. Thick lenses on his frameless glasses magnified his eyes and spurred on his closest friends to nickname him Mantis.

"What's going on here?" he asked.

The front doorbell rang before there was any chance for an answer. Dr. Armitauge, Oliver Brandt, and the Tenzios were on the front step.

"Hey Mike, Stacy. Everything okay?" Carter asked.

"Can we come in?" asked Stacy. She wiped her eyes with a tissue. "We have to talk to you guys about a couple of things."

"Absolutely." He bent a wary eye toward the two strangers.

Soon seven people stood around Griffith's dining room table.

"First of all, let me introduce Dr. Arthur Armitauge and Mr. Oliver Brandt," Mike began. "They are here to help us."

"Help you with what?" asked Molly.

"Get Kita back."

"Get Kita back!?"

"She's been kidnapped."

Molly looked at Amanda.

Amanda nodded her head.

Mike began. "We found out this week that Kita has some unusual abilities and because of those abilities, some bad people were out to get her. Because I was slow to understand the magnitude of things explained to us by Dr. Armitauge, Kita has been kidnapped and I put Amanda in grave danger. Please forgive me, Amanda."

"It's not your fault, Mr. Tenzio."

Molly kept looking at Amanda. "So you *are* the copper-haired girl the police are looking for?"

"Police?" her dad asked.

Then words burst from Amanda in a torrent. She detailed everything: Elliot, the tiger eating the frozen chickens, the zoo animals escaping, Longstreet and the cigarettes, Ja'el in WWII, Adrienne, the evil astral, the kidnapping, the shooting, and how Oliver saved her life.

During her entire explanation, her parents kept glancing over at the Tenzios as if they were expecting them to stop the nonsense pouring forth from their daughter. When she was finished, Dr. Armitauge tried to conceal a smile, Mike was amazed at Amanda's recall, Stacy was crying again, and Molly and Carter Griffith were speechless.

"I think we should all sit down." Molly opened her palms to the empty chairs.

"Mr. and Mrs. Griffith I realize this all sounds a bit fantastic," Dr. Armitauge began, "but I assure you, Amanda has recounted the events with amazing clarity. I must impress upon you that it is highly possible they will make another attempt on her."

"I'm sorry." Carter Griffith stood up. "You realize all this is totally insane, right?"

"Mom," Amanda said, "remember at the zoo when we did the video. How Elliot came up to the glass and posed and how Kita was laying against me? That's when she was in there talking with him and telling him what to do. She had to lay against me because when she is traveling her physical body acts like it's sleeping."

"I do remember thinking that more was going on there then I was aware of. But this —"

Stacy stood up behind her husband and put her hands on his shoulders. "Maybe at some other time we can do the convincing of what Kita can and can not do but we have more important things to consider. Doctor, please tell us your plan. We will follow your advice this time."

Mike shook his head in silent agreement.

"If Kita is the one with abilities, why would they want Amanda?" Molly asked.

"Coercion," Oliver answered. "If Kita won't cooperate they might use the threat of doing harm to Amanda, to get her to do what they want."

"I think I know what they want," Amanda said. "They want to use her like they do the other one. I think whoever kidnapped her is into secrets and blackmail. His empire is built on information no one else can get or information no one wants public. Because he can be invisible, and be anywhere, he can get information others can't."

Dr. Armitauge placed his hands on the table. "When did you figure this all out?"

"It's all I've been thinking about since I got home."

"You are an exceptionally insightful young woman," said the doctor.

"There's one other thing too. They want the book."

Dr. Armitauge looked over at Oliver. "I told you."

"Told him what?" asked Molly.

"He told me your daughter was brilliant," Oliver answered.

"Actually, I told him a bit more than that. I am not only an old man, but I am ill. By my own diagnosis, I am surely living the final year of my life. For most of the long history of the astrals, there has always been a Sentinel."

"A what?" interrupted Amanda's dad.

"The Sentinel guards the Book of Ciphers and is the keeper of the ring. The Sentinel is also a protector for the astral and keeps her physical body safe when she travels. The Sentinel must be chosen by the astral and they have a forever bond. Amanda, I am hoping you are willing to become Kita's Sentinel. In the ancient past many of the sentinels were chosen for their physical strength or personal wealth. Adrienne chose me because I'm her uncle and please excuse my lack of humility but she also chose me because of my intellect, and Amanda my dear, your intellect is formidable."

"How would you know this about me?" asked Amanda.

"School records are all electronic now, susceptible to hacking. IQ of 153 and your intuition is even greater than I had hoped. Come back to the island with me. You will be totally safe and I can begin to teach you the ways of the Sentinel."

"First of all," Carter Griffith broke in. "I don't trust someone who has broken into the school files to snoop on my daughter. On top of that, this isn't some decision she gets to make. We're her parents and we'll be the ones deciding if she runs off to some island. Besides, you can't expect a fourteen-year-old girl to make a decision that will set the course for her whole life! That doesn't even include that you're expecting us to let go of her based on some wild fantasy fiction you're spewing out!"

"Actually Dad, Joan of Arc was advising the French armies when she was fourteen. King Tut was rebuilding Thebes when he was fourteen. Alexander the Great was thirteen when Aristotle was tutoring him and he colonized his first city when he was sixteen. Jordon Romero climbed Mt. Everest when he was thirteen and at fourteen Mozart already had his operas being performed by the best professionals in the land."

"Well, you're not one of them," her dad shot back.

"Actually, Mr. Griffith, I think she is," the doctor answered. "One other item you should consider: any schooling Amanda wants, anywhere she wants, will be totally paid for, complete with private tutors, if she wishes, and around the clock security.

"It's not fantasy fiction either!" Amanda declared. She rose to her feet. "Dr. Armitauge, I'll do anything to help get Kita back but doesn't Kita have to choose me first to be her Sentinel?"

"Think about it, my dear. Kita has already chosen you." Dr. Armitauge smiled and placed his weathered hand on top of Amanda's

Chapter 20
Ile Brouillard

Even after some intense arguing between Amanda and her parents, followed by serious pleadings from Mike and Stacy, the Griffiths were still not keen on letting their youngest daughter go off with complete strangers but they were wavering. It was Oliver Brandt who finally got them to relent.

"If I may interject for a moment." He handed his card to Carter Griffith.

Oliver Brandt
Commander USN
Special Agent: Homeland Security

"I am sorry for what Amanda had to witness today. I promise you, that if you permit her to join Dr. Armitauge, I will be her personal bodyguard 24/7. I will give my life before I allow anything to happen to her."

"What's this special agent business?" Molly had taken the card from her husband's hand.

"I am on loan to the doctor and Adrienne. The things they do are of utmost importance to the security of this country. Amanda is not being asked to join up with some crazy, superhero run around. She will be entering into a sacred service not only to her country but to freedom and peace-loving people everywhere. We have stopped wars, prevented the spread of nuclear weapons, brought down wicked warlords, halted genocide, and have been instrumental in the mediation of strong treaties. Not to mention what we have done to human traffickers, organized crime, poachers, major polluters, and corrupt officials. Yes, this decision will set the arc for the rest of her life but that arc will be one of distinctive merit that few people could ever hope to earn."

A thoughtful quiet descended on the room when he finished.

Finally, Molly reached for Amanda's hand. "You call me every night."

"I will, Mom." Amanda gave her the bear hug of bear hugs.

* * *

A small airstrip was nestled along Lake Superior on the northeastern tip of the Red Cliff Reservation. Dr. Armitauge was given free access to the airfield ever since he had helped the tribe win a financial settlement from the state of Wisconsin. A classic 1936 Chris-Craft Cabin Cruiser was waiting for them at the dock of a small marina just minutes from the hangar.

"Wow!" Amanda exclaimed as she stepped on board.

The deck's deep mahogany woodwork, the original instrument panel, and the chrome in the lounge shone with a polished luster.

"I'm glad you approve," Dr. Armitauge said with a smile. "I have owned this boat for fifty-eight years and have had the luxury of keeping it perfectly ship-shape."

A low rumble vibrated through the hull when Oliver started up the twin inboards. Those engines roared once the boat cleared the breakwater. Amanda faced backward, mesmerized by the flowing wake. It was a clear night. The Big Dipper blazed enormous and bold above the horizon. Her gaze followed an imaginary line on the outer edge of the ladle up to the North Star. They were heading east.

"Where is the island?" asked Amanda.

"Thirty minutes out," Oliver said.

"There are over twenty islands in this area but because of the twelve largest ones, a French cleric, Xavier Charlevoix, gave them the name, Apostle Islands," Dr. Armitauge explained. "The natives have individual names for the islands and my little island is tucked between Anweshin-nigig and Ziinzibaakwado."

"Does your island have a name?"

"When I first came to see this island it was shrouded in fog so I named it 'Ile Brouillard,'"

"I suppose that means fog island?" Amanda said.

"Maybe we will teach you French as well my dear. You seem to appreciate its beauty already."

Oliver pulled back the throttle and the boat slowed to a gentle troll along the west side of the island. Steep stone cliffs jutted forty feet straight out of the water. The boat hugged the wall, slowing even more. Then Oliver cranked the wheel and they eased into an opening in the massive wall. The roof of the boat's cabin barely cleared the limestone arch. Motion-activated lights came on and flickered across the moist walls of the natural cave. Oliver brought the boat to a gentle stop alongside a man-made wharf. He hopped out and secured the bow and aft with double braided dock lines. The trio ascended a staircase hewn out of the rock that led to a paneled hallway. At the far end, a solid oak door swung open before them and they entered the great room. Amanda had to raise her head to take in the high peaked ceiling held up by gigantic log beams. Two rocking chairs with padded cushions faced a wall of glass. A massive stone fireplace with a timber mantle dominated the opposite wall and three sofas formed a U around a huge tabletop created from the cross-section of an ancient white pine. However, what commanded Amanda's attention was a ten-foot-high portrait. The woman was stunning. Her black hair was swept back by a breeze. Piercing hazel eyes that almost glowed, bored into all observers. Fog swirled around her legs and behind her. She wore no clothes. Instead, she was covered with a grayish, silvery bodysuit with deep blue flecks. It covered her face, ears, arms, hands, everything.

"Is that Adrienne?" Amanda asked.

"No, that is Evelyn," Dr. Armitauge answered. "The most incredible creature to ever walk the face of the earth."

"But how—?"

"Did we do the painting?"

"Yes."

"It is a self-portrait. She used a mirror and memory. I made many requests over many years before she finally agreed to do it."

"But when Kita looked in the mirror she was invisible."

"It is one of the things you will learn about the ring."

"She is beautiful," Amanda added.

"Yes, she was."

Another man entered the room. He was slightly taller than Arthur and a bit heavier but there was no mistaking they were brothers. They could have passed for twins.

"Amanda, this is my brother, Francis."

Francis lifted Amanda's hand, then lowered his head to kiss it.

"It is my pleasure to know you. I am thrilled that you have agreed to come. You honor us with your presence." His crisp English retained a hint of his French heritage.

Amanda blushed.

"I am quite tired my dear child. I must retire," Dr. Armitauge said. "Oliver will show you to your quarters. We will eat breakfast at 8:00 and then begin."

Francis slung his arm around his older brother and the two old gentlemen strolled out of the great room.

"This way." Oliver carried both of Amanda's bags.

Her room was wood-paneled with a row of high windows. Plush carpet went wall to wall. A bed, two chairs, lamps, a desk, and a small table were spaced out neatly around the room. She had a private bath and a walk-in closet.

"I hope you will be comfortable," Oliver said.

"How could I not be? This is really nice"

"Well, goodnight then."

"Can I ask one question before you go?"

"Sure."

"Was the doctor in love with Evelyn?"

"You'll have to ask him that I'm afraid. You do realize she was quite a bit older."

"I know, but —"

Oliver smiled at her before he quietly closed the door behind him.

Chapter 21

Antiquities and Alphabets

A few minutes after Bayne's private jet lifted off from refueling, Kita drifted off to sleep. She woke a couple of hours out from Melbourne. Wrancor was staring at her.

"You're a bad person," she said.

"Bad? I'm just following orders."

"You kidnapped me and punched me in the mouth with your gun. You shot at that man. I'd say you're pretty bad."

"You know nothing about me."

"I know enough."

"Maybe, but I know a more about you."

"Oh yeah, like what?"

"You're looking for a woman named Adrienne. You've only been traveling a few days, so you don't really know what you're doing, and you have two glaring weaknesses."

Kita stared at him. It was an angry, hate-filled stare.

"You have a silly love for animals and you'd do anything so your friend Amanda wouldn't get hurt."

"Where is she. If you hurt her I'll —"

"You'll do what? You really are a hot-tempered little Sheila, aren't you? I also met that gorilla friend of yours. I don't like him very much. I think in a week or so when I have some free time I might go back and end him."

Kita sprang from her seat and landed on Wrancor's lap. Both her knees dug into his legs. She slammed her fist into his shoulder, square on the bloodstain. She got in four furious blasts before he threw her onto the floor.

"Why you little twerp. I warned you." He pressed his knee in her back and grabbed a handful of hair. "Napier, get back here!"

The SUV driver hurried into the cabin.

"Help me tie her down."

When she was completely strapped down, Wrancor gagged her and put a bag over her head.

"I warned you."

Then he tied a rubber tube above the elbow on her left arm. She started squirming but her arms had been strapped down in three places. Wrancor took a syringe out of a small leather case and found a vein. He plunged the needle and emptied the contents.

"This ought to take care of you for a while."

In minutes, Kita's eyes closed, her chin sank to her chest, and her breathing was slow and steady.

* * *

Amanda was seated at the breakfast table at 8:00 am sharp. Glimpses of the lake peeked through the towering pines. The sun was up and a slight breeze turned the surface of the great blue lake into thousands of sparkling diamonds. Dr. Armitauge was sipping his coffee. A short, rotund man came through the door. He placed a plate on the table in front of her with scrambled eggs, French pastries, and fresh pineapple.

"Thank you," she said.

"This is Enrique," the doctor said. "He is our chef and he is most excellent."

"Hello, Enrique. I'm Amanda."

"Of course. I know this Miss Amanda. Welcome to Ile Brouillard. It is my honor to know you. Any special dish you want, you tell me." He lifted her hand and kissed it.

"You guys sure do a lot of hand-kissing," Amanda remarked.

"In my upbringing, it is the proper way to greet a woman of distinction," Dr. Armitauge said.

Amanda blushed.

"Where are Oliver and Francis?"

"Oliver is refueling the boat. Francis is currently speaking with Boyd and Malek in Australia. They haven't made contact with Adrienne yet. We are getting worried."

"You have people there?"

"Two. I may have to go there myself. I don't know yet, but not today. Today you and I shall begin."

"What's first?"

"This morning will be the alphabet and antiquities. This afternoon you will meet with Oliver."

"Oliver?"

"I will be doing the academic training and Oliver the physical."

"Physical?"

"He will teach you how to defend yourself and how to take care of your body."

"But I hate Phy-ed."

"You might not like this either, at first."

Amanda attacked her food while Arthur sipped his coffee, eying her. When she was finished, he stood.

"You were hungry."

"Famished."

"We have our work to do now. Please come with me."

Amanda followed Dr. Armitauge through a short hallway and

down a wooden staircase. At the bottom was a small room with a stone floor, thick wood paneling, and no furniture. Arthur walked up to a square glass panel on the opposite wall and put his face a few inches from the glass. The panel lit up. A narrow green beam of light scanned bottom to top, left to right. When it was finished, the entire wall disappeared into the floor. A second wall was hiding behind the first wall. It was made of stainless steel.

The doctor spoke into a microphone embedded in the wall next to a vault door. "A.A. underground one."

This wall also disappeared into the floor. They stepped across the threshold and the steel wall rose up behind them. Amanda tuned into the sound of a compression seal when the wall finished closing.

Smooth, terra cotta colored ceramic tiles covered the floors, walls, and ceiling. The only furniture was a conference table and four chairs. Two wooden boxes were at one end of the table. One box was the size of a small suitcase and the other was so small it could fit in Amanda's hand. A hollowed-out stone held mechanical pencils and some pens. Two note pads sat next to the pen holder. There was a chrome cylinder in one corner of the room with a pebble-sized green light that blinked on and off every ten seconds.

"Let's sit down, shall we?" Arthur pointed to the chairs.

After they had been sitting for more than a minute, Amanda finally asked, "When do we start?"

"We already have."

"I don't understand."

"The greatest learning springs forth from curiosity. You have seen quite a lot in the last twenty-four hours and no small amount in the last five minutes. You have questions. Ask anything you want and let's see where that leads us."

"Where does all the money come from?" Amanda asked. "This island must have cost millions."

"As does our enemy, we trade in secrets as well. However, we are not into blackmail and extortion. We lend our services to the CIA, FBI, State Department, the military, law enforcement agencies, and occasionally, for certain organizations. As Oliver explained to your parents, when our work is done, bad guys go to jail, lives are saved, and countries find peaceful solutions to their conflicts. We are paid handsomely. Plus, my brother Francis is a financial wizard. Let's just say he has invested wisely over the years."

Amanda pointed to the walls and ceiling. "The insides of this room seem strange to me. There are no outlets, no switches, and it's like everything is the same material."

The doctor smiled. "You really are quite observant Amanda. You know how Kita can travel through walls and glass?"

"Yes."

"There is one material an astral can not pass through. It is ceramic made from a special clay called ultisol. The science and geography of all that can come later. For now, realize this room can not be penetrated by an astral. We have total privacy."

"Can I look inside the box?" She pointed to the larger one.

Dr. Armitauge slid the box to her side of the table. There was no hinge. Amanda lifted the top and set it on the table. There were three items inside.

"May I?" Amanda asked.

Dr. Armitauge handed her a pair of surgical gloves. "Put these on please."

"Why the gloves?"

"They prevent the oils on our hands from damaging the items."

First, she removed a ceramic tube almost two feet long. Three stones that looked like diamonds were encased on one end. Two were glowing amber and one was glowing blue.

"How is it possible that these gems are glowing?" she asked.

"Absolutely no idea," he answered. "But I do know what they are for. As you know there can only be at the most three astrals on earth at the same time. The gems keep count. When a gem glows amber it is for an astral bent for good. Blue is for an astral bent for evil."

"So, Kita and Adrienne are the amber and that guy from Australia is the blue."

"Yes. For a number of years, it was two blue and one amber. Then one of the blues went out and it was one and one. Thirteen years ago when the other amber gem lit up, we knew there had to be a Kita."

Amanda turned the tube over and over. She tried untwisting one end. Then she tried pulling the top off. Nothing worked.

"How do you open this?"

"You can't. It can only be opened by an astral. When they push the gem that glows for them, the top slides off."

"Inside?"

"A scroll. It tells the astral history from the beginning up to the fifteenth century and contains instructions on how an astral can strengthen their abilities and how to use the ring. The last person to write on the scroll did so before Christopher Columbus was born."

"Wow. I've never seen anything this ancient before, let alone hold it in my hands."

Amanda placed the tube back and pulled out a book. It had a leather cover with strange symbols carved on the front. The pages were of the thinnest leather Amanda had ever seen. They were not bound like a normal book. Every page had five holes on the inside edge and were held together with a leather cord. Amanda examined each page. They contained symbols that looked like the ones on the front but they were in columns and across from each column was a column of letters from even more languages Amanda did not recognize.

"That is The Book of Ciphers. Tell me what you notice about the columns."

"They are in pairs. The first column in every pair is the same."

"Very good. Any ideas?"

"You did say I would be learning about alphabets today. My guess is that one language is being translated to others. Like a codebook. There are only five pairs, so five translations?"

"Excellent! Yes, five and each is an ancient language no longer in existence. The keeping up with languages lapsed. It is why I got my PhD in ancient languages. I kept studying until I found an alphabet that matched one in the book. I did the French translation. As far as I know, I am the first Sentinel in centuries to access the scroll."

"What about that original language column?"

"That's the astral language that only they can read. The great mystery is that they don't have to learn it. Somehow, they can read it the first time they see it."

"That must be the language on the scroll then."

"Right again. It is only through the Book of Ciphers that the Sentinels can learn the ways of the astral and how to serve them. Without the Book of Ciphers, nothing I will teach you today would be possible."

The third item was one page only. It was protected in a plastic film. It only had one column pair.

"French?" Amanda asked.

"Yes."

"What about English?"

"Turn it over."

Amanda turned the page over. A neat double column ran down the page. There were 41 symbols. Some were translated to a letter and some into a word or short phrase, all in English. She examined the translation for a few minutes.

"The memorization will come later," Dr. Armitauge said.

"Is the ring in the small box?"

"Open it and see."

Amanda fumbled with the little box. She couldn't even find where it opened.

"I suppose I can't open this either?"

"You can but it is a puzzle. I'll show you the first step."

Dr. Armitauge slid a sliver of wood on one side of the box and handed it back to Amanda. She looked over the rest of the box trying to find a seam for the next piece to slide.

"Try it with your eyes closed," the doctor suggested.

Amanda closed her eyes and ran her fingers across the surface of the box. She found the next thin veneer piece and slid it open.

"Five more and you have it."

It took her ten minutes. The seventh piece didn't slide, it had to be pushed. When she did it, the box opened. Inside was the ring. It was a band not quite a half-inch wide with three symbols carved on the surface.

"Is it gold?" Amanda asked.

"I don't know what the material is. I have run a variety of tests on it and can not identify it as any substance found on earth."

"How do you explain that?"

"I can't."

"What are the symbols for?"

"Each symbol represents a special power an astral can perform when they're wearing the ring. The first symbol that looks like a lightning bolt represents the ability to melt metals."

"Like turn metal into liquid?"

"With extreme heat. The range is about thirty yards. There is an ancient story in the scroll about an astral who melted the swords and shields of a horde of barbarians invading her village. The invaders ran off in great pain from being scorched. The villagers collected the metal after it had cooled and re-forged it for themselves."

"Wow! What about the middle symbol? It looks like an upside-down triangle sitting on its twin."

"Time displacement."

"What's that?"

"The astral stays in normal time. But no time passes for those around her. The first time Evelyn showed us this, Francis, Marie, and I were in the same room. The next thing we knew, Evelyn was in a different chair, eating a sandwich, and sipping on a cup of coffee. She had placed a flower in my lapel, set Francis's hat on his lap, and took Marie's shoes off. It happened in a blink and we didn't know it."

"That's incredible. So, Kita could do that if she was wearing the ring?"

"If she was trained. And we have found the effect lasts only as long as they can hold their breath."

"That's weird."

"I agree."

"The last symbol?" asked Amanda.

"Paralysis."

"Really?"

"If two astrals are close enough to one another to touch, the one with the ring can paralyze the other. It is a sure way an astral can be defeated in battle. As long as the wearer of the ring hangs on, the other astral remains paralyzed. This power can only be performed while traveling. The other two can be done with the physical body or the astral body."

"Why doesn't Adrienne wear it all the time then?"

"She does wear it on special assignments. But it can never be lost, so it is not an everyday accessory. Oh, Amanda, one more thing. Very important. Never, ever, put it on."

"Why?"

"It will turn your hand to dust."

Amanda placed the ring back in the box as if it was a deadly spider.

Chapter 22
Granddaughter

Bayne's private airstrip was on the west edge of his property, a mile from the main house. The plane taxied to a stop inside the hangar. The steps lowered and Bayne climbed aboard, Cerberus at his side.

"What's wrong with her?" Bayne pulled the bag off her head and the gag out of her mouth. Cerberus sniffed her legs and hands.

"Nothing. She attacked me so I put her out with a little morphine. She'll come around in a bit," Wrancor answered.

"Why did she attack you?"

"I think it was something I said."

"I told you not to hurt her," Bayne reminded him. "What if she overdosed, you idiot?"

"I didn't hurt her. I just made her quiet. I gave her less than a third of what I take. She's a feisty little Sheila; quick temper this one. If I hadn't drugged her I might've had to hurt her."

"I work with imbeciles." Bayne pointed for the door. "The doctor is waiting for you in the hangar."

Bayne stuck his head out the door and motioned at two men who were standing at attention by a black Tahoe. "Take her back to the tower. Put her in the west room and make sure she stays put. Take Vulcan with you. Text me if he barks."

One of the men carried Kita and laid her in the back seat. They both hopped in the front and drove off.

"Now things will start to get interesting," Bayne told Cerberus as he scratched him behind the ears.

* * *

Adrienne went outside when she heard the plane coming in. She went back to her room, laid on the bed, and traveled to the hangar. She floated to the side of the building, making sure to remain out of Cerberus's sight. Bayne entered the plane. A minute later, Wrancor stepped out and went directly to the office hangar. Adrienne lowered herself just outside the window and watched as a doctor removed Wrancor's shirt. She saw the bullet wound in his right shoulder. The doctor cleaned the wound with green beta-dine and gave Wrancor a shot. He waited a couple of minutes before he poked him in the shoulder with a sharp needle. There was no reaction. He used a long, slender tweezers and pulled out the bullet.

"Let me see it," Wrancor said.

The doctor held it up.

"Wash it off. I want to save it."

"Souvenir?"

"Something like that. How bad is the wound?"

"You're going to be sore for a few days. We'll have to keep an eye out for infection but I think you're going to be okay. You'll probably have to do some rehab on the shoulder. You have some damaged muscle tissue in there."

The doctor swabbed more disinfectant on the wound and stitched him up.

Adrienne floated over to the plane and peeked through a cabin window. Kita was slumped down in one of the seats. Adrienne's heart melted when she saw her. Kita's thick hair and dark complexion reminded Adrienne of her daughter, Dawn. She wanted to hold her, help her, and protect her. As she continued gazing at Kita, another emotion welled up within Adrienne.

Anger.

"This is not going to end well for you, Mr. Bayne," she whispered to the wind.

Bayne cut Kita's restraints and gave orders to two men. They carried her off the plane and put her in the back seat of a large SUV and drove away. Adrienne remained out of sight while Bayne and his dog walked to the hangar office. Then she went skyward until she saw the SUV that was carrying Kita. In a breath, she was hovering above the roof. She stayed there the entire twenty-eight miles into the city.

Kita was still out cold when the SUV entered the private underground parking ramp of Eureka Tower. One man carried her and the other let a Rottweiler out the tailgate. Adrienne hid behind a support post until they entered the elevator. She hovered below the elevator's floor until it reached the top. When it stopped she went outside the building and peered through a window. The dog was searching room by room but never looked outside. Adrienne went around to the side of the building that allowed her to peer in on Kita. The men closed the door on their way out. They left the dog inside the room.

Adrienne waited.

* * *

Kita started moving. First, she rolled her head back and forth a few times. Then she opened her eyes, stretched her arms, and rubbed her hand on the side of her jaw where Wrancor had clubbed her with his pistol. It was swollen. She looked at her inner elbow and rubbed the spot where the needle had delivered the sleeping potion. She sat up when she spotted the dog.

"What's your name?" she asked.

Vulcan remained motionless. His eyes locked in on hers and he let out a low, rumbling, guttural, growl.

Kita always had an instant rapport with animals; not this time. She remembered Mtotah's warning, "Not all animals are good." The dog's nasty expression added to her already growing fear.

The bed and a small table with a lamp were the only furniture in the room. Three of the walls were bare but the third wall was glass from floor to ceiling. She went over and stared out the massive window. She didn't know she was in the top apartment on the tallest building in Melbourne but she knew she was sky high and was awed by the view. Suddenly, the Rottweiler was next to her and barking at the window. Seconds later he turned sharply and started growling at the opposite wall as if someone was there.

Then Kita also remembered, "watchers."

She hurried over to the bed, laid down, and came out.

Two seconds after she hit the bed, the taller of her two guards stormed into the room.

"Vulcan. Silence!" He sent the text he'd been ordered to send, then examined Kita lying on the bed. "She's still out cold you goofy mutt." Vulcan kept up his barking. The man dragged the dog out of the room.

There she was.

Her body was bright penny copper, with dark streaks that swept down the side of her face, onto her neck, and over her shoulders. Her hair was dark bronze, and her eyes were a clear forest green. The end of her fingers were talon-like, and she looked young, nothing like a grandmother.

Kita didn't have to ask if it was Adrienne. She knew. She slowly floated over to Kita and gave her a long embrace.

"Let me hold you," she said.

Kita was surprised she could feel Adrienne's arms and body.

"I didn't think we could feel anything when we traveled," she said.

"My darling girl. Yes, we can feel each other. You can't imagine how I have waited for this." Adrienne stroked Kita's face. "I'm so sorry about all this. It is all my fault. I didn't want to meet under these circumstances."

"You're my real grandmother then?"

"Yes." She squeezed Kita tighter. "But, I don't even know your name yet."

"It's Kita."

"It's a lovely name and strong."

"It's the name Dawn gave me."

"You know about Dawn?"

"I know she was my birth mother, that she got sick and died, and that she didn't tell you how you could find me."

"Well, I have found you now."

"Where are we?" Kita asked.

"Let's go outside and have a look."

Adrienne rose about fifty feet above the building and Kita followed.

"This city is Melbourne. The apartment you're in belongs to a bad man that we're going to have to deal with."

"The evil astral? I met him. He's the one who kidnapped me?"

"No, that's Colton Wrancor. He works for a man named Bayne. Bayne is the one who owns this apartment."

"Does he have you captive too?"

"Yes. My body is at a station north of here."

"A station?"

"That is what they call a ranch here in Australia."

"How did this Bayne find me?"

"I'm not sure but probably the same way Arthur found you."

Kita thought about kids posting videos of the dogs emptying Longstreet's backpack. *Maybe revenge isn't always the best idea after all*, she thought to herself.

"What's going to happen to us?"

"I'm not exactly sure how but we are going to get out of this. I will be back tonight. I know that today's traveling will have made my body weak. I will have to go back and rest. We'll meet right here."

"How will I know when?"

"You'll hear Bayne's dog barking. Then Bayne will come in and check on you. Tell him you were snooping around trying to figure out a way to escape. When he leaves, come out and see me here."

"Okay." Kita kept hanging on to Adrienne's arm.

"Are you afraid Kita?"

"A little."

"I won't let anything happen to you. Bayne will try to intimidate you; try to get information out of you. Act as ignorant as you can. He already knows about the doctor and me. However, don't tell him we met, don't tell him about the ring, and don't tell him you know there can only be three astrals."

"I won't."

Adrienne kissed her on the forehead and was gone. Kita went back to her body, got off her bed, and walked out into the apartment. Vulcan was waiting just outside the door.

He followed.

The men stood up when she entered the main room. One was slightly taller than the other. They both had neatly trimmed hair and were lean and muscular. Each one wore a shoulder holster with a gun. They stared at her. She stared back at them. Vulcan stood at attention.

"Where am I?" she asked.

"Does it matter?" the shorter one answered.

"What time is it? There aren't any clocks."
"It's four in the afternoon."
"I'm hungry," Kita announced.
"You're going to have to wait."
"For what?"
"Not for what, for whom."

Chapter 23

Wealth and Power

"Give him something for the pain but don't knock him out. I will need him shortly." Bayne said as he entered the hangar office.

"I'll give him another local then," the doctor answered.

"How serious is it?" Bayne asked.

"He'll recover but he will need therapy to regain full use of that shoulder. Right now he needs rest."

"Very well. You can leave us now. A car is waiting outside."

The doctor gave Wrancor another shot, then packed his things, and strode out to a black BMW. The driver tossed his cigarette on the ground and squished it with the toe of his boot. Then he slid into the front seat and started the car.

"You can go up to the house and rest," Bayne instructed Wrancor. "but I need your *presence* at the tower this evening. We'll leave here at seven. I'm going to question the girl. I'll need you to tell me when she's lying."

* * *

The two guards snapped to attention when the elevator door opened and Bayne and Wrancor entered the sky view apartment. Wrancor went straight to his room. A few seconds later Vulcan barked but stopped when Cerberus growled at him. Then Cerberus tapped his nose on Bayne's leg one time. Bayne patted him on the head.

"Go get the girl," he commanded. "then go back out to the station. Take Vulcan with you."

"Yes, sir," they both said.

"The kid says she's hungry," the shorter one said.

"I'm sure she is."

The guard barged into her room without knocking. He didn't bother asking her to come. He just grabbed her by the arm and started pulling her to the door.

"You don't have to drag me," Kita said. She yanked her elbow from the guard's grasp. "I'm coming."

She stopped struggling when she saw Bayne and Cerberus. She couldn't decide which one looked meaner, Bayne with his baldhead and ugly scar, or the dog that was pure muscle with a menacing snarl in his eyes.

"Have a seat, Miss Tenzio." Bayne pointed to one of the leather chairs.

She sat.

"Cranston tells me you're hungry. What would you like?"

"I'd like to go home."

"A sense of humor with a streak of sarcasm. I like that."

Kita didn't answer.

"Whether or not you ever go home again will depend on your level of cooperation. For now, you're here. If you don't want to eat, that's up to you."

Kita's hunger outweighed her stubbornness.

"What do you have to eat?" she asked.

"Anything you want."

"In that case, I'll have a thin crust pizza with pepperoni and green olive."

Bayne pulled out his phone. "I'll have my Tuesday night usual. I also want a thin crust pizza with pepperoni and green olive."

Bayne poured himself a bourbon and sat facing Kita.

"Let's you and I have a pleasant conversation, shall we?" Bayne began. "Or, if you prefer, I can employ some 'motivational techniques' that will improve the clarity of your communication."

"Is that why I'm here, to talk?" Kita asked.

"Among other things."

Kita thought about the time she was called to the principal's office after she had poured super glue all over Ben Longstreet's bike padlock. Amanda had instructed her to say as little as possible and ask questions of her own. She wasn't interested in finding out about Bayne's 'motivational techniques,' so she decided to see where this talking would get her.

"You know my name, what's yours?" she asked.

"You can call me Mr. Bayne."

"Why did you kidnap me?"

"I need you for some projects I have in the works."

"So, if you need someone you just go and kidnap them?"

"Sometimes."

"I don't like you."

"I didn't expect you would. Now let's not waste time pretending you don't know why you're here. You have special abilities that are of value to me. You can cooperate with me and we could use them together. If you choose that path, you would become a very wealthy young woman and have the freedom to come and go as you please. You could even see your parents again. If you don't cooperate, I have means to force your compliance. They are not pleasant means. If neither one of those work out, I could arrange to end your traveling altogether."

Kita said nothing.

"So, how long have you been able to travel?" Bayne asked.

"I've only known about it for a few days. I did it once when I was little but I thought it was a dream."

Bayne looked at Cerberus. He made no motion or sound.

"What do you know about Adrienne?"

"An elephant told me about her. She's a traveler too."

"Anything else about her?"

"I think she might be my real grandmother."

Nothing from Cerberus. Kita noticed that after she answered a question, Bayne would steal a quick glance at the dog. *A watcher dog*, she thought. *Maybe Wrancor was in the room too.* Kita felt herself tensing up.

"What would make you think that?" A little smirk creased Bayne's face.

Kita realized she shouldn't have said anything about Adrienne being her grandmother. She was afraid Bayne was better at asking questions than she was at answering them.

"The elephant said I looked like her and she had seen her many, many years ago."

Cerberus nudged the side of Bayne's leg.

Kita noticed.

"Let's try that answer again," Bayne said. "You know more than that."

A horrible realization swept through Kita. For all she knew, Wrancor could have been watching her long before she was kidnapped. How else would he have known about Elliot being her friend?

Her mind raced.

He couldn't have been at her house when Dr. Armitauge visited. She would have seen him. He wasn't at the zoo either but how did he know where to find her and Amanda? Then she remembered the walk home the day before she was kidnapped. She had told Amanda everything about Dr. Armitauge's visit. It would be horrible if Wrancor heard all that.

She left her body.

Cerberus barked.

Wrancor was hovering next to him. He grinned a slimy grin and tried to grab her.

She went back. She'd only been out for a second.

Cerberus stood and barked at her again.

"Find what you were looking for?" Bayne asked.

"Your guy's here," Kita answered. "But I suppose you already knew that."

"I did know that. You still haven't truthfully answered my question about your grandmother."

Kita remembered Adrienne's instructions. The ring, their meeting, and the existence of only three astrals could not be mentioned and he already knew about the doctor.

"I'm adopted. But a man came to my house and told me about my real mother and about Adrienne."

Cerberus was back in his stoic, silent position.

"That wasn't so hard was it?"

"I really, really don't like you."

Bayne chuckled.

"Not many do," he said. "Now let's talk about possibilities. I'm in the information business and as you probably have already guessed, I can have someone sitting in on the most secret of meetings, making the information I gather, shall we say, very valuable."

"If you already have your other guy, why do you need me?"

"With two travelers at my disposal, I could double my profits and increase my power. I'm interested in more than just Australia."

"What will you do with more money and more power?" Kita got up and stood beside her chair.

"Such a naïve question young lady."

"Looks to me like you got a real nice place here already. You have enough money to hire people to come halfway around the world to kidnap me and fly me back on a private jet. What do you need, another apartment? Another plane? Do you even have any friends? Or do you just have people who let you boss them around because you pay them? Or maybe the only reason they stay is that you threaten them like you're doing to me. You need more people to boss around, is that it?"

Bayne scowled at Kita. "You know nothing about wealth and power. You're just an ignorant, smart-mouthed, little girl. There are people in this country who delude themselves into thinking they are powerful but those same people show deference to me. I have the real power because I know their secrets. I have bankers, lawyers, and politicians who, when I call them, they do what I say. But that's only Melbourne, Canberra, and Sydney. I want New York, London; even Moscow. Secrets are a powerful weapon."

"I may be ignorant as you say I am, but I have people who love me and care about me. You can keep your kind of wealth. I don't need it."

"If you already have those people, wealth won't cause you to lose them. You can have both."

"If they found out how I got my wealth, they might not think so much of me anymore. So, I guess I don't really want to work for you. Their love is more important to me than your money."

Bayne took a long swallow on his drink and studied the defiant, dark-haired girl standing before him.

"Your choice," he said.

Then a bell chimed by back elevator in the kitchen. Bayne pushed a button on a small black remote control device sitting on the lamp table.

"The food is here but since you're not interested in cooperating, let's see if being hungry changes your mind."

An older man with a slight limp came out of the elevator. He was pushing a food cart.

"Place my dinner on the table," Bayne said. "Take the pizza back with you. We won't be needing it."

Then he turned to Kita.

"Go to your room. I eat alone and you don't eat at all."

* * *

Colton Wrancor not only listened to see if Kita was lying but he listened to the other things she said as well. She was right that Bayne had no friends and that his employees all hated him. They only followed his directions out of fear or greed. He didn't care for Bayne all that much either but he loved the money and all the things it could buy. Family? Friends? Love? He'd never needed any and couldn't figure out why this Kita kid thought it was so great. He let Cerberus know he was going back to his body.

Chapter 24

The Hole

Standing in front of the wall of glass in her room, Kita watched the sun set behind the city. Her conversation with Bayne had her worried. The only thing holding her together was the thought that Adrienne was coming in the night. Kita was confident she would bring a plan to get them out of this mess. She wanted to go home. She wanted to see Amanda. She wondered if Mahshando had been moved to the preserve yet. She even started wishing she was a normal person.

Then Bayne entered her room. He had two men with him. They were not the two guards who had been with her earlier. These two were older, rougher. They each grabbed one of her arms.

"What do you want now?" Kita said.

"I've decided to provide accommodations for you that more closely match your level of cooperation."

One of the men taped her mouth with duct tape. The other man wrenched her hands behind her back and bound them with a zip tie.

Kita struggled and tried to scream but it was useless.

Then Bayne held a horrid looking metal collar in front of her face. It had many spikes pointing upward on the outside rim. There was dried blood on a few of the tips.

"This is a little device I developed when Colton went through his rebellious period as a young teenager. He didn't always want to do as he was told either." Bayne held the collar a little closer. "This cured him of disobedience. It will give you second thoughts in case you get the idea of traveling. If you keep your head upright, you'll feel no pain. However, if your head nods one way or another, you will find the pain quite exquisite. If your head nods the wrong way for too long, I'm afraid the blood loss would be rather substantial."

He tried to wrap it around her neck. Kita squirmed and shook her head. One of the men grabbed her hair and held her head in place. Bayne encircled the collar above her shoulders. There was a click that sounded like something locking. He nodded and the man let go of Kita's hair.

Kita slowly moved her head to one side. Her movement was met with a horrific stab of pain. She moved her head in another direction and felt the same piercing pain.

"It won't matter which way you turn, pain awaits your every move. Best stay awake."

Bayne took a picture of her with his phone and then nodded to one of the men. The man tied a blindfold over her eyes.

The men led her by the arm to the elevator. She sensed the elevator dropping and felt the cool air when the door opened in the underground garage. She worked hard at keeping her head steady as the men jammed her into the backseat of the car. The car went slow at first, made some turns, and then it sped up. Kita thought they must be on a highway. The fast driving lasted twenty minutes. Kita counted. Then the car slowed down again. There were three more turns and they came to a stop. They opened the back door.

"You can get out. Watch your head now," one of them said in a joking voice.

Both men laughed.

Once in the house, they led her down a flight of stairs and pushed her through a doorway. They took off her blindfold, pulled the duct tape off her face, and undid her hands. It was just the two of them, no Bayne. The room was smaller than Kita's bedroom back home. It had no furniture, no lights, and no windows.

"What about this thing?" Kita asked. She pointed to the torture device on her neck.

"Hate to tell you this little Sheila but we don't have the key for that."

They laughed again as they closed the door on their way out.

Kita heard the unmistakable sound of a deadbolt sliding into place.

Total darkness. Total silence.

She started running her fingers over the choker collar. It was feeling heavier by the minute. She counted ten super-sharp points thrusting up from the base. There was about an inch of space between the razor-like tips and her chin and neck. She tested the sharpness of one of the spikes. The pain from pricking her finger gave her all the info she needed. Next, she walked the outer edges of the room and placed her hands on all four walls. They were covered with a dense foam-like material. She shouted. The sound died into the walls. She willed herself to stay calm but when she realized not a soul in the world knew where she was, her control gave way to panic. Oh to be back in that world where Ben Longstream and Harry Warthog were her only problems. She'd never felt so helpless, or so alone, or so afraid.

She cried.

"I hope you're not crying for my sake." It was Bayne's voice coming through a speaker in the ceiling. "Just so you know, I also have Adrienne in my custody. I purposely left Adrienne unattended when your plane landed. I figured she'd follow you to the tower. I'll bet you two have already talked. But now she doesn't have a clue where you are. I have a special collar for her also. You see Kita, I know how to control things. I know how to get what I want and I never lose."

"How am I supposed to sleep with this thing on?"

"Oh, you won't. When you're screaming in agony. When you're on the verge of going insane. When you're begging me to take it off. When you tell me you'll do anything so you don't have to wear it anymore, then I'll let you sleep…and eat."

"I hate you!" Kita screamed.

There was no answer.

Kita remembered a story she had read in school about how prisoners of war in Vietnam kept from going crazy by concentrating on a few simple things that meant a lot to them and not allowing those things to ever leave their memory. It was their anchor to reality. Kita started focusing on Barney and Goldie, her rabbits, her turtle, her birds, Mahshando, Amanda, and of course, her mom and dad. She willed herself to see their faces and remember their sounds. She went through them one by one. She would not move on to the next one until she had a secure memory about the one she was concentrating on.

Her legs and feet started to hurt from standing. She edged her way to a wall and sat down, making sure to keep her neck clear of the daggers. She struggled to find a comfortable position. She couldn't rest her head against the wall without getting poked. Looping her thumbs inside her belt helped stabilize her body. An idea crept her way, a flicker of hope. If she was in total darkness, Bayne couldn't see her. She removed her belt and wrapped it around her neck, like a shield between her skin and the blades. She stabbed her hands a couple of times doing so but she managed to buckle the belt and cover her neck. Then she took off her shoes and socks. She rolled her socks into tubes and stuffed them at the back of her neck, between the belt and the points. She leaned back for a test run.

No pain.

Then she laid on her back. She pushed her shoes together like a makeshift pillow. She rested her head on them, hoping the shoes would keep pressure off her neck.

Still too much pressure.

She took off her pants, rolled them loosely, placed them atop her shoes, and tried again.

All was good.

She nestled her head down a bit to form a depression so her head would stay in one place. She was able to lay there with no pain.

Then, she was out.

Hovering above the roof, she scanned all directions. The night sky had settled in. Across a bay, Melbourne's skyline looked like towering fortresses with beaded lights that shimmered over the water. She dropped to the street level. Her house of captivity was a normal house in a normal neighborhood: 12 Chisholm Place.

She memorized the address and how to get back. Then she raced across the bay. She wasn't sure exactly what building was Bayne's. She went to the tallest one first and looked in the windows of the top apartment. She'd guessed right. Bayne was seated at a desk looking at something on his computer. She waited. Adrienne arrived in less than half an hour.

"Why are you out here already?" she asked.

"They moved me. I'm in a house over there." Kita pointed back across the bay. "I'm in a room in the basement with no lights or windows. Bayne put this horrible collar around my neck. It has super sharp points sticking out so if my head goes too far in one direction, I get cut."

"Show me."

They flew back to the neighborhood and hovered outside the house.

Kita explained to Adrienne how she used her belt and clothes. "He said he has one for you too. There is a speaker in the ceiling. That's how I hear him when he talks to me. He said he will leave that collar on me until I cooperate."

"How long have you been out here?"

"I'm not sure but I'd say about an hour."

"I'm going to check the situation inside. I'll back in a second."

Adrienne filtered through the outside wall and returned in a few seconds.

"There's good news and bad news in this situation," Adrienne said. "We would have had a horrible time trying to get you out of the tower but this house we can deal with. There are only two guards in there. So Bayne must be talking to you through his computer back at the tower. The other thing you should know is that when you are traveling, you feel no sensations from your physical body. However, when you go back in, all feeling comes back. So if your body is in pain now you are going to feel it when you get back."

"That's not the bad news?" Kita asked.

"The bad news is I need you to go back. If Bayne starts talking to you again, I need you there. He can't know we've discovered his plan. You have to act like you never left."

"But I hate it in that room and that collar thing is driving me crazy."

"I only need you to hold out for a little while."

"How long is a little while?"

"Couple of hours at the most. Can you do that?"

"I think so. What are you going to do?"

"I'm going to get you out."

"How?"

"I was lucky on my way to the tower. I finally found the men that Arthur sent for me."

"How did you find them?" asked Kita.

"They send up an infrared beam at night. You see, when we travel, if we focus we can see infrared light. However, during the day there is so much of it that a single beam cannot be distinguished from all the rest. At night a beam can be spotted. There has always been a plan in place that if a rescue would be needed, the rescue team would identify their location by activating the beam. I have been traveling around Melbourne the last few nights. Nothing. I'd given up hope. But tonight on the way here I saw the beam. There's hope."

"But how will you communicate with them?"

"Through the dog."

"Really?"

"I'll have to show you that later."

"Okay."

"When it happens it will happen quickly. Two men will come for you. What's your favorite pet's name?"

"Barney."

"They'll use that word so you know they can be trusted. Be brave my little Kita. I have to go." Adrienne hugged her and flew off.

It was the first time in her life that Kita didn't mind being called 'little'.

When Kita returned to her body, her homemade armor was still working. She slipped back into her pants, put her shoes on, and went back to leaning against a wall.

"You aren't talking to me anymore?" Bayne's voice descended through the speaker.

Kita wasn't sure how long he had been trying to talk to her so she chose her answer carefully.

"I'm trying to ignore you."

"Are you going to answer my question?"

"Which one?"

"Are you ready to cooperate yet?"

"I don't think so."

"Why do you want to torture yourself? Just a simple little task I have for you. The collar comes off and you can have something to eat and drink."

"You're the one doing the torturing, not me."

"I'll check back in when you start screaming." Bayne sneered. "The job I have for you isn't ready for a few days anyway. I'm in no hurry."

Chapter 25

Extraction

Mark Boyd, Collin Malek, and Riga had been in Australia for four days. The exact coordinates that Arthur received on his phone led them to Moolap, a little area southeast of Geelong. They stayed there for two nights setting up the infrared beacon each night. After conferring with Arthur, they moved north of Geelong and when nothing happened, the fourth night they headed for Melbourne. They chose a high spot in Panton Hill northeast of the city and set up camp. Like Oliver, they were both highly trained, both extremely fit, and both on loan to Dr. Armitauge from one of those branches of a branch of a branch embedded deep in the labyrinth of U.S. Intelligence.

At exactly 10:17 Riga gave two sharp barks and nudged Boyd in the leg.

"She's here," he told Malek. "Get the pad out."

Malek removed a flat rubber mat from the back seat and rolled it out in the bed of the pick-up they were driving. The mat looked like a giant computer keyboard. Each key was the size of a playing card. At the bottom were three rows of keys. Instead of letters, they contained commonly used words. The mat was connected to a computer.

Riga jumped up to the bed and began pressing keys.

Need immediate extraction! Kita is at 12 Chisholm Place in West Melbourne. Two guards. Safeword is Barney. Hurry!!

"What about you?" asked Boyd.

Get her to the island. Come for me later. I'm at a ranch north of the city. It has a hangar. Now go!

"Okay, we're on our way."

They rolled up the mat, put Riga in the back seat, and took off. Malek googled 12 Chisholm Place.

"Is that empty pizza box still in the back?" asked Boyd.

"Yeah."

A half an hour later they drove by the house one time and then parked the truck facing outward in the dead-end street. Both men twisted silencers onto the end of their guns. Boyd pulled a gray, Kangol baseball cap over his hair, tipped the brim sideways, and slipped into a loosely fitting beach shirt. He grabbed the pizza box and headed for the front door. Lights were on in two of the inside rooms. Malek slid through some bushes and peeked through a window. He held up two fingers and went to the back. When Boyd's phone vibrated in his front pocket he knew Malek had unlocked the back door. He rang the doorbell. A light came on and one of the guards looked out a narrow window on the side of the door. Boyd held the pizza box flat in one hand and his 9mm hidden underneath it in the other.

The guard opened the front door.

Stupid and untrained, Boyd thought.

"We didn't order a pizza. You got the wrong place, mate."

Boyd dropped the pizza box and grabbed the man's collar. Before the box hit the ground the muzzle of his gun was firmly planted on the guard's forehead.

"On your stomach, hands behind your back," Boyd commanded.

When the man was on the floor, Boyd clamped his wrists with zip ties and stuffed a hat in his mouth. He pulled the man's gun out of the shoulder holster and slipped it inside his own belt behind his back.

The other guard rushed in from the backroom and reached for his gun. He froze when he felt the tip of Malek's silencer at the back of his head.

"Hand it over, nice and easy," Malek instructed.

The guard handed it over. Malek pulled out the clip, emptied the chamber, and tossed it onto a chair. Then he delivered a swift, crushing blow to the back of his head. The man crumpled to the floor.

"Take us to the girl and you live. Force us to look for her and who knows." Boyd used his toe to nudge the man laying at his feet.

He offered no resistance. "She's downstairs."

"Lead the way." Boyd grabbed him by the back of his shirt collar and lifted him to his feet, never letting the tip of his gun break contact with the back of the guard's head.

The guard led them to Kita's prison. He unlocked the deadbolt and opened the door. Boyd stepped forward and whispered, "Kita. Barney sent us to get you."

Kita ran to him.

"We'll get that barbaric thing off you when we're on our way but now we have to go."

Boyd turned his attention back to the guard. He held up a small disc about the size of a dime. "If you make any sounds in the next half hour the vibration from your vocal cords will activate the chemical in this pin. Believe me, mate, you won't want that acid on your skin." He taped it to the back of the guard's neck.

Malek bound and gagged the guard he had knocked out upstairs. Two minutes later the pick-up was speeding toward a waiting plane at Avalon Airfield.

"Is that thing you put on that guy's neck really have acid?" Kita asked.

"No. It's just a used up watch battery but the illusion works all the time."

The lock on Kita's torture collar was electronic. Boyd used a miniature screwdriver to loosen a small panel on the back of the collar. He clipped a wire. There was a soft click and the lock on the collar came undone. He swung open the hinge on the front and removed it from Kita's neck. He held it up for her to see. The barbs were welded to the side of the ring. Some fresh blood covered crusty bloodstains that had been dry for a long time.

"This thing is disgusting," Boyd said. "Stop the car for a minute."

Malek pulled over to the side of the road. Boyd got out, slipped around to the back, and pulled a heavy hammer out of a toolbox. He set the collar on the tar and pounded it into crumpled mass, breaking off every blade.

After he finished demolishing the collar he sent a text to Arthur.

EXTRACTION COMPLETE. ON OUR WAY.

* * *

Two hours had passed since Bayne had last talked to Kita. He was getting perturbed that his young captive wouldn't talk to him, hadn't started calling for help, or begging to be released. He was beyond upset when his men at the house wouldn't answer their phones. He was in full-blown outrage when he drove to Chisholm Place and found both men bound and gagged with Kita gone.

"This means war!" he roared.

Cerberus stood at the ready.

Chapter 26

Negotiations

Mike Tenzio came running into the kitchen when he heard his wife screaming. She was crying. She handed him her phone. He read the text from Dr. Armitauge.

WE HAVE HER. SHE'S SAFE. BRINGING HER TO THE ISLAND.

Mike relaxed when he realized Stacy's tears were all joy.

"What should we do?" he asked.

"We're going to stick with the plan. Stay put and act normal. Zach can keep staying with Derek and Brenda until we get the all-clear."

"But I want to see her," Mike objected.

"We'll see her soon enough."

* * *

Bayne unbound the gagged guard, splashed water on his face, and slapped him a few times. He was groggy and confused when he finally came to.

"What happened?" Bayne demanded.

"Someone came to the front door with a pizza. When I went to check, a second bloke had his barrel at the back of my head."

"What did they look like?"

"I only saw the bloke who took down Burke. He looked like a pizza delivery guy."

"Idiot," snapped Bayne.

"They knew the girl was here." the guard said, keeping his gaze at his feet.

"Figured that out all by yourself, did you?"

Bayne barked orders into his phone. "Bring the woman and Wrancor to the tower!"

Then Bayne turned to the two guards. "You go wait for me at the station. I will deal with you later."

Bayne slammed the door on his way out.

* * *

Two men entered Adrienne's room without knocking. She knew things were in motion now.

"Come with us," one of them commanded.

Adrienne had seen these two together before. They were the two with Wrancor when she was originally captured. She had determined they were Bayne's best. Still not highly trained but better than the rest she'd observed. If she were younger she would have taken them out without a second thought. It had taken her three years to earn her black belt in jujitsu. It had taken many more years to perfect her skills. But now, her age, and the weakening of her body, and because of the guns they were carrying, she decided she would follow them to the car. Wrancor was in the back seat. His arm was in a sling.

"How's the shoulder?" she asked as she slid in next to him.

"Very funny. I'm not done with that little hothead. She'll wish she'd never laid a hand on me."

"What little hothead are you talking about?"

"Bayne has your precious little Kita. I'm pretty sure the way she spends the rest of her life is going to depend on you doing exactly what he says."

"Good to know," Adrienne said.

"He didn't get where he is by being a nice guy," Wrancor added. "He knows how to get what he wants."

"Is that how he gets what he wants from you? Fear? Is that why you're his lapdog?"

"I'm not afraid of anyone and I'm nobody's lapdog."

Adrienne turned toward him and raised an eyebrow. "Whatever you say."

The foursome walked out into the main room of Bayne's apartment when the elevator door opened. Bayne was waiting. His fingers were tapping the arm of his chair.

"You can sit." He pointed to a sofa. Adrienne and Wrancor sat on opposite ends.

Adrienne scanned the room. She knew the bourbon on the cabinet table was at least $500.00 per bottle. The leather on the furniture was lamb's skin. She examined the painting above the mantle. It was by Frederick Remington of a Native American mounted on his horse, hiding behind a rock formation, with his rifle trained on an unsuspecting covered wagon.

"Nice painting," she said. "Original?"

"Obviously. It's called Apache Ambush. I like the spirit of the scene."

I'll bet you do, Adrienne thought to herself.

"I'm done playing games with you." He handed her his phone. The picture was of Kita with the death collar around her neck. "You will do what I want or that girl is going to go insane trying to keep from stabbing herself to death."

"You have shown me this picture and you have told me you have the girl but I'm not sure I believe you. You haven't let me actually see her."

"You have no choice but to believe me."

"Let me see her or talk to her and then we can negotiate."

"We're going to negotiate now or I'm going to lengthen the barbs on that collar."

Adrienne realized Bayne used threats when he was bluffing. She also realized that his bluffing meant there was an extremely high probability that Kita had been rescued.

"What exactly do you want me to do?" she asked.

"I want the book. Get me the book and I will let her go."

"And what about me?"

"I'll decide about you after I have the book."

"I'll trade the book but it will be for my freedom only."

"But what about the girl? She's your granddaughter. Isn't that a bit negligent?"

"As I said, show her to me or let me talk to her. If you really have her then that might change things."

"Not happening," he said. "She's too far away."

"Nice try with the photo but I don't believe you have Kita."

"Believe me, I have her."

"Prove it to me and I'll deal."

"Aargh." Bayne rose to his feet. He stood in front of Adrienne. His face reddened. He fingered his cigar lighter with one hand and waved a finger in her face with the other. "You're really pissing me off, lady!"

"At least you didn't call me Sheila."

Wrancor snickered.

"You think she's funny do you?"

Wrancor straightened his face.

"My offer still stands," repeated Adrienne. "My freedom for the book."

"You're willing to give up the book too easily. A trick maybe? Earlier you said you would have to physically go and get it. I'm not letting you do that."

"There is one person I can call who can have the book delivered."

"Who might that be?"

"He will remain anonymous and I make the call on a burner phone, not one of yours."

"Wait." Wrancor jumped to his feet. "It is a trick. The book is written in some ancient traveler language and it can only be read if you are wearing some special ring."

"What are you talking about?" Bayne turned his attention to Wrancor.

Adrienne sized up Wrancor. He looked sleazy and lazy to her. She was sure he had no martial arts training, just an irresponsible playboy punk who used his talent as a mercenary to live the soft life. *Bayne wouldn't want to have him fully trained*, she thought. Too dangerous.

Adrienne's body slumped against the back of the sofa and she was out.

Cerberus barked.

"After her!" screamed Bayne.

Wrancor went limp and tore out in pursuit.

He didn't have to go far. Adrienne was waiting behind the sofa. In an instant, she was on him. She grabbed one of his thumbs and twisted his hand and wrist with a violent wrenching. He screamed in pain. With her other hand, she pressed her thumb in an eye socket. He was immobilized and hurting badly. She dragged him up to the roof. Although her physical body was deteriorating, her astral body was as strong as ever and her jujitsu training was still fully available.

"Didn't know you could feel pain while traveling did you?"

He tried to pull himself free. It only made his pain worse.

"Keep struggling and I'll increase the pressure." She pushed harder into his eyeball to make sure he understood the fullness of her intent.

"Okay. Okay, I'm done!" He held himself still.

"I'm going to ask you a few questions," Adrienne said. "If I think you're telling me the truth, I'll let you go. If I think your lying, well just so you know, I'm only cranking at half throttle."

"I get it."

"How do you know about the ring?"

"The day before we kidnapped the kid I overheard her conversation with the copper head girl."

"And?"

"Some old guy had to give her a ring so she could read some letter from you."

"What else do you know about the ring?"

"Nothing."

Adrienne increased pressure.

"Nothing. Nothing, I swear!"

"You're not much of a thinker are you?"

"What do you mean?"

"Why do you think Bayne wants the book so bad?"

"I've never thought about it."

"Like I said, not much of a thinker."

"If you're so smart why don't you tell me," Wrancor sneered.

"He thinks the book will tell him how he can control me. But more importantly, he thinks the book has the secrets that will give him total control over you as well. He's constantly worried about keeping you under control. Without you, he's nothing. If you decided to actually turn on him, he knows he couldn't stop you."

Adrienne felt Colton's resistance wane. She was confident the thought she had just planted in his mind was doing its work.

"The book is the only reason he hasn't killed me yet," she continued. "Come to my side, Colton. We can take him down."

"I'm on nobody's side but my own. Besides, you can't take him down. In case you've forgotten, you're his prisoner, he's not yours. You have no idea of the extent of his network. He's got people everywhere. I'm going back."

Adrienne cranked up the pressure.

"Ahhhhg!"

"Can you feel that?"

"Yes."

"One more thing, not only can you feel pain when you travel, you can die. Not that many years ago I was forced to end an astral. He thought he was invincible. He wasn't. I'll do it again if I have to. Are we clear?"

"Clear," he cried.

She let him go.

Once back they both sat upright at the same time. However, Adrienne found herself bound to a hard wooden chair. A collar just like Kita's had been strapped to her neck. Rubber tips covered each razor-edged point.

"Back so soon," Bayne sneered.

He walked to Adrienne and pulled the rubber tips off, one by one.

"Now you will only travel when I say so. Get my point?" He laughed at his own joke.

Colton looked at the collar and smiled. "Told you."

"So you did."

Chapter 27
Colton Wrancor

Colton Wrancor was born in the outskirts of Sydney to a teenage girl who gave custody to the state with two stipulations. She wanted to remain anonymous and she wanted the boy taken far from Sydney so his father would never find him. Colton passed through more than one foster home. None were willing to adopt. When he was five, one set of foster parents took him to see a psychiatrist because he wouldn't stop claiming he could talk to animals and fly in his sleep. They became more concerned a year later when two strange dogs were fighting in the backyard while Colton sat watching all the action. Their concern turned to fear a month after that when Colton had been sent to his room for hitting his foster sister.

"I'm going to send my dog after you," he threatened.

They didn't own a dog, so they weren't sure what he was talking about. However, when the foster dad went to get in his car for work, a Doberman came straight for him. He didn't bite. He just barked, growled, and wouldn't let him get to his car. They took Colton back to the foster agency the same day.

Within a month he had made many enemies and spooked all the foster workers at the agency. He heard them whispering to themselves about the strange boy who would sleep for hours at a time and could not be wakened. Five weeks in, a man named Mr. Bayne came for him. Colton was afraid of him at first. The man talked nicely but Colton could tell he didn't mean it. He didn't like the jagged, sinister-looking scar on his neck either.

His new home was so outside his experience, it was beyond his imagination. It didn't take him long to like his own room with his own television, his own bathroom, and his own collection of video games. He could use the swimming pool anytime he felt like it and if he went into the kitchen, the cook would make him whatever he asked for. Orturo, an aboriginal man with wrinkled leathery skin and white hair taught him how to ride and care for horses. He was the only person on the entire grounds that Colton trusted.

Colton ran to the back of the house one day when he heard a plane landing on the airstrip. A huge man ambled down the stairs of the plane and was driven to the house. An hour later Bayne came to the horse barn to fetch Colton.

"There is someone who is ready to meet you," he said.

"Is it the man who came in on the plane?" asked Colton.

"I see you're paying attention to what's going on around here."

Bayne escorted him down a hallway to a set of double doors. Men wearing suit coats were stationed on either side. Colton had not seen these two before. They looked even scarier than the other gun-carrying men who patrolled the station. One of them opened the door when Bayne and Colton approached.

The man sitting behind the enormous desk was enormous himself. His fingers were as big as sausages and his loose-fitting linen suit had enough material to build a tent. He was lighting a cigar when he waved them forward. He set a solid gold cigar lighter on his desk. It was shaped like a huge bullet and tiny diamonds formed V.N. on the edge. A large Rottweiler sitting at his side started to move toward Colton.

"Sit, Ajax!" the man commanded.

On either side of the doorway were two gigantic paintings of naked women eating fruit and drinking from golden goblets. An even larger painting of a solitary aboriginal hunter with his spear and boomerang hung behind the desk. A leather cord kept the hunter's hair out of his face as he scanned the barren outback. He looked like Orturo with a white beard.

"Sit here boy." He pointed to one of the chairs on Colton's side of the desk. "Claude, I want to talk to the boy alone."

Bayne scowled at Colton and left the room.

For the first time, Colton learned Bayne's first name.

"Have you been treated well?" the man asked.

Colton nodded.

"You don't have to be afraid of me, boy. I'm here to take care of you, not hurt you. My name is Mr. Newsome. You can call me Vincent. Everything you see here, the house, the barns, the animals, the people, it's all mine. You can live here as long as you like. Would you like that?"

Colton nodded again.

"Good. Now we have something very important we need to talk about."

Colton looked at him blankly. He wasn't sure if he was supposed to answer or not.

"Have you left your body since you've been here? Have you talked to any of the animals?"

Colton froze. He'd been out of his body once and talked to the horse he'd been riding. He didn't want to say anything because he was sure he would get in trouble all over again. So, he didn't answer.

Vincent Newsome smiled.

"I am glad you know how to travel. It's a good thing. You have my permission to travel anytime you want."

Colton had never heard anyone describe what he could do as traveling. He always assumed something was wrong with him and he shouldn't be doing what he was doing. He remembered the psychiatrist saying things like delusional, psychotic, and post-traumatic. He had no idea what those words meant but he was sure they weren't good. He couldn't understand how this man could know about him and he was still confused about what was real and what wasn't. However, even in his six-year-old mind *traveler* made sense. And this man seemed to think talking to animals was okay.

"Once," he finally answered. "I wanted to talk to my horse."

"Very good. What did you talk to him about?" Newsome asked.

"His name and how old he was."

"What did he say?"

"His name is Tobias and he's many moons old. I don't know what that means."

"Moons are like months," Newsome explained. "Anything else?"

"He likes it when I ride bareback better than with a saddle."

Newsome chuckled and slapped his meaty hand on the desk. "Well, bareback it is then."

For the first time in his life, Colton was relaxed about his abilities and didn't feel like he was some sort of freak. He even permitted himself to smile; something he never did.

Newsome stood up and walked over to Colton and placed his thick slab of a hand on his shoulder. "Colton, as long as you live with me you can travel anytime you want. I only ask two things. First, I want you to come and tell me where you went and what you saw or heard. Tell only me, no one else, not even Mr. Bayne. I never want him to know what you can do. Second, don't ever travel to where I am unless I ask you to. Do we have an understanding?"

Colton nodded. Newsome held out his hand but Colton didn't know what he was supposed to do.

"Shake my hand boy. It shows we have an agreement."

Colton allowed his hand to disappear into Newsome's massive paw.

* * *

Except for Bayne always lurking in the background, for the next four years everything was great. Colton lived the life of a spoiled child. He traveled where and when he chose. He always reported to Mr. Newsome. The only real 'work' he had to do, were lessons designed to increase his memorization skills. They were taught by Bayne.

"Why do you think Mr. Newsome wants you to increase your memory skills?" Bayne asked one day.

"I don't know. He's never told me."

Two days after that he found out when he was summoned to Vincent's office.

"I have a special job for you today, Colton."

"What is it?"

Newsome turned his computer screen so Colton could see. There was a picture of downtown Melbourne. The cursor was focused on one building.

"This is the Grand Hyatt in downtown Melbourne. You've traveled downtown a few times right?"

"Yes."

"Good. Two men are meeting in room 817. I want you to go there and listen in on their conversation. Remember all that you can and then come straight back here."

"How long should I stay?"

"The most important thing is if they say anything about money. I really need to know about that. Stay as long as they are together then you can come back."

"Should I go now?"

"Now."

Colton sat back in his chair. In moments he was hovering over the men in room 817. He wasn't sure if he got the right information but when he told Newsome that one man gave the other man $50,000.00, Vincent smiled and patted him on the shoulder.

"Excellent job, Colton. There's a reward waiting for you in the machinery garage."

It was a dune buggy.

Overnight everything changed. After breakfast, he was told Bayne wanted to see him in Mr. Newsome's office. Bayne was standing behind Vincent's desk smoking one of Vincent's cigars. He slipped Vincent's gold cigar lighter into his front pocket.

Colton could not figure out where Mr. Newsome was or why Bayne had his lighter.

"Do you know what this is?" Bayne pointed to a thin disk a little smaller than a quarter.

"No."

"It is a battery-powered receiver/transmitter. The most sophisticated listening device money can buy. It has been on the recessed light up there for a couple of weeks." Bayne pointed to a light directly above Vincent's desk. "Vincent died last night and I'm taking over his operation."

"How did he die?"

"Heart attack I'm sure. He was terribly overweight and I don't think these cigars did him much good."

"He was fine when I talked with him yesterday."

"Most times these things just happen without any warning."

A deep worry and uncertainty gripped Colton. He felt a tightening of his throat and a churning in his stomach. He always sensed Vincent protected him from Bayne. He didn't like the idea of Bayne being the new authority in his life. Although he was only eleven, he was smart enough to know that if Bayne had been listening to the conversations in this office for two weeks, he knew all about Colton's travels, especially yesterday's.

"What does taking over the operations mean?" Colton asked.

"From now on, you report all the details of your travels to me. And we continue your memorization drills."

Colton's special assignments increased. By the time he was fourteen, he had figured out how Bayne was using the information he gathered. He also learned the hard way that Ajax was a watchdog. He decided to see what Bayne was up to one night when a stranger arrived at the house. Ajax started barking as soon as Colton was hovering in the room. He flew back to his body. Seconds later Bayne was in his room with two guards. They strapped a hideous looking collar around his neck.

"From now on you only travel when I tell you to and where I tell you to!" Bayne snapped. "There are ten points of interest that will poke holes in any ideas you have of traveling without my permission."

Colton was stubborn and mad. The collar didn't come off for three days. When it did, he and Bayne came to an agreement. Colton obeyed Bayne in return for money and toys. Although Colton loved all the money and all the toys, he never lost his resentment. And every time Bayne used Vincent Newsome's cigar lighter, that resentment flamed to all-out hatred.

When Ajax died, Bayne used a sports car to bribe Colton into training a Rhodesian ridgeback named Cerberus and a Doberman named Vulcan.

Chapter 28
Adrienne Sends a Message

Barney and Goldie were jumping at Kita's legs when she stepped onto the hidden wharf of Ile Brouillard. Kita laid on the ground and let them have their way. They wouldn't stop licking her face and crawling all over her.

"I brought them with me when I came, just in case," Amanda said. She hugged Kita extra long when she finally stood up.

Dr. Armitauge performed all the introductions. Kita couldn't believe how much Francis and Arthur looked alike.

Then she remembered.

"You're my great-grandfather, aren't you?"

Francis smiled and kissed her hand. "Yes, child, I am."

"They do a lot of hand kissing around here," Amanda explained.

Kita looked at Oliver. "I thought you were a magazine reporter?"

"That was my cover story so I could keep an eye on you two. Please forgive me for not protecting you."

"I know you tried your best. I saw what you did to those three guys. With just a few more inches you would have had Wrancor too."

"It is necessary for you to rest," Dr. Armitauge said. "A few hours of sleep, a good meal, and then we will get started."

"Get started?" Kita asked.

"You have much to learn and time may be of the essence."

* * *

"Colton, tell me about the ring," Bayne said.

"All I know is that the girl needed to wear the ring to read the ancient language. It's what she told the copper headed girl."

"Is this true?" Bayne turned to Adrienne.

"If you want to read the book, you'll have to wear the ring. My offer still stands, we'll just have to include the ring."

"Oh we will, will we?" Bayne snorted.

Colton chuckled.

"Here's *my* offer," Bayne said. "I get the book and the ring. If I like what I read, you live. If I don't like what I read, you don't. It's that simple."

"What guarantee do I have that I live even if you like what you read?"

"You don't. But like I said when I first met you, I want to use your abilities. Working for me will ensure you live."

"Working for you is out of the question."

"Really? A few days in the collar and you'll be surprised at what you are willing to do."

Adrienne looked over at Wrancor. His face was blank. She realized that at one time he'd probably worn this collar too.

"For now we're going to make a video and you're going to tell me the number where I can send it," Bayne said.

* * *

"Time to get up." Amanda softly shook Kita's shoulders.

"I'm still tired. Give me one more hour," Kita complained.

"No, we have to get going," Amanda insisted.

A groggy Kita followed her to the dining room. She perked up when she saw the table spread out with lasagna, salads, fruit, bread, cheeses, and tiramisu.

"What do I have to learn first?" Kita asked after the second helping of her favorite dessert.

"First the ring, then the vault," answered Dr. Armitauge.

The five of them walked into the great room. The ring was on the giant white pine tabletop in the middle of the room.

"Lesson number one," Dr. Armitauge began. "is to learn how to command the ring to come to you."

"What?" Kita asked.

"Stand where you are and focus your mind on the ring. Focus on the *idea* of the ring leaving the table and coming to your hand."

Kita held out her hand and concentrated. She tried blocking everything out of her mind except the thought of that ring. Nothing happened.

"Focus," Amanda encouraged.

Kita tried imaging the ring lifting off the table and coming to her hand. But the ring didn't budge.

"It's okay." Dr. Armitauge picked up the ring and handed it to Kita. "Let's do the symbols and come to this later."

Kita slipped it onto her thumb. She felt that thrilling rush of power she'd felt the first time she wore it. The feeling of power went beyond physical. Somehow, her awareness of everything around her was heightened as well.

"Why did you choose the thumb?" asked Francis.

"I thought it would fit best there."

"Try your other fingers."

Kita placed the ring on each finger. She watched in amazement as the ring resized itself to fit perfectly on each different finger.

"That is awesome!" exclaimed Kita

"But the thumb is the best," Dr. Armitauge said. "It allows you to operate the powers with one hand."

Kita moved the ring back to her thumb.

"Now let me show you the three symbols and how to use them. The one that looks like a lightning bolt is for melting metals. But you must be extremely careful. You don't want all the metals around you to melt. If you focus your eyes on one place, only the metals in that area of focus will melt. Let's try it."

He placed a stainless steel serving spoon on a block of old wood.

"What exactly do I do?" asked Kita.

"Use your zoom vision so only the spoon is in your line of sight. Then touch the symbol and keep focusing on the spoon."

Kita zoomed in, then touched the symbol. As she did, the spoon turned to a molten puddle and smoke smoldered off the wood slab.

Amanda clapped. "Yea!" she hollered. "First time!"

"Next, I want you to push the symbol that looks like an hourglass and hold your breath. I can't explain why but the amount of time you can hold your breath is the length of time the rest of us are in suspended animation. Try it and play a couple of tricks on us if you can."

Kita touched the symbol and held her breath. Francis, Amanda, Oliver, and Dr. Armitauge became motionless. Kita stared into Amanda's eyes. She waved her hand in front of her face.

There was not even a blink. She held her ear close to her Oliver's nose. There was not even a breath. She put Dr. Armitauge's glasses in her shirt pocket and slipped out of the room before she exhaled.

"She's gone!" Amanda exclaimed. "Did she disappear?"

"No, I'm right here." Kita walked back into the room. She handed Arthur back his glasses.

"Well done, Kita," the doctor said.

"What is the one that looks like a diamond do?" Kita asked.

193

"That one is a bit more complicated. You don't have to push it to make it work but as far as we know it only works when you're traveling."

"But what does it do?"

"If you grasp another traveler when you are wearing the ring they become paralyzed for as long as you hold on to them. There is no way to test it so we only know about it through what is written in the scroll and what Adrienne told us when she had to use it."

"Scroll?" asked Kita.

"That will be part of the vault lesson."

"When did Adrienne have to use it?" Kita asked.

A look of grave concern overtook Dr. Armitauge. "She had to end the life of an evil astral once."

"She did?"

"There was a time before you were born when Adrienne was working on a human trafficking case in Thailand. While listening in on some corrupt officials, she was confronted by a male astral. Because of the scroll, she knew he existed, but it was apparent to her that he had no idea she existed. She tried talking to him but he became angry and attacked her. A mistake on two levels. Adrienne is highly trained in jujitsu and she had the ring."

"What happened?" Amanda and Kita asked at the same time.

"Let's just say it did not end well for him, but it ended."

"Oh, I think Adrienne was telling me about that," Kita remembered.

"I want you to try the command the ring to come to you one more time. Only this time I'll have you do it while you're outside your body. Hover next to the fireplace and command the ring to come to you."

Kita did as she was told. Hovering by the fireplace she concentrated on the ring as before. Suddenly the ring flew off the table and into her hand. The rest of the room exploded in applause when the ring disappeared from their sight.

"Now come back into your body and see what happens," Dr. Armitauge instructed.

Kita came back and the ring stayed on her finger.

"Excellent. Now let's try it again. This time as you are."

Kita placed the ring on the table and walked over to the fireplace. She held out her hand and concentrated. The ring was in her hand in an instant. There was no applause this time. Instead, there was a silent sense of awe.

* * *

Arthur was surprised when the text alert went off on his phone. He was horrified when he watched the video. He called everyone into the communications room. He plugged a cord into his phone that allowed the video to be displayed on a large screen. Francis, Kita, Amanda, and Oliver stood and watched as the picture of a bound, collared, and gagged Adrienne filled the flat panel.

The voice was Bayne's. "As you can see your associate is in a rather uncomfortable position. In exchange for her life, I want the book and the ring. Yes, the ring. I know I can't read the book without the ring. You have 36 hours to deliver both to 12 Chisholm Place. I believe you know where that is. There will be no negotiations. I get what I want and I let her live. That's the deal."

The screen went blank.

For thirty seconds there were five silent stones standing in the communications room.

Oliver was the first to speak. "Play it once more."

Arthur pushed the arrow.

"Look!" Oliver pointed to Adrienne's hands. Her wrists were strapped to the arms of the chair but her hands were free and she was tapping her fingers. "Once more," Oliver repeated. "And get me a pencil and paper."

Arthur played the video again and Oliver started writing.

"I get it!" exclaimed Amanda.

"What?" Kita asked.

"Morse code."

Oliver wrote the letters as Adrienne tapped them out. Amanda peeked over his shoulder. s.e.n.d.i.t.s.e.n.d.i.t.

"Send it," Amanda said. "She tapped it twice."

"The ring?" asked Francis. "How could he have ever found out there was a ring?"

"Maybe he got it out of her somehow," offered Oliver. "Or maybe she's desperate."

"She would never tell him," Arthur said.

"Then how?"

"I don't know but we have to get her out," Francis insisted.

"But we don't even know where she is," said Oliver.

Kita finally spoke. "Play it one more time Dr. A."

They all watched once more.

"She's in Bayne's apartment at the top of the tower. I don't know the name of the building but it is the tallest in the city. It's where he kept me before they took me to that house."

"What is the thing around her neck?" Amanda asked.

"It's a torture collar. If she travels and her head goes limp, she'll get stabbed by those blades sticking up. He put one of those things on me. It's horrific."

"It still doesn't answer our main question. What is the meaning of Adrienne's message?" asked Francis.

"The plane trip is eighteen hours, plus another hour to the house," Oliver said. "That doesn't give us a lot of time. We better figure out why she's okay with us sending the ring and come up with a plan."

"I think I might know what she's thinking," Amanda said.

"Tell us what you think," Dr. Armitauge motioned to Amanda. "You have the floor."

"Kita, you said Colton threatened to harm Elliot. That means he'd been hanging around us a while. He probably listened in on our conversation when you told me what happened when Dr. A visited your house and how you needed the ring to read the message. Adrienne is telling us we're okay to send it because that's all Bayne knows about the ring. He doesn't know what will happen to him if he puts it on. He said in the video he knows *he* has to wear it to read the book. She *wants* him to put it on. He's keeping her in the tower because it is his most secure place. Plus, he doesn't know that we know where she is."

"But I don't get it," said Kita. "why would she want Bayne to wear the ring?"

"Because," Amanda answered. "if a non-astral puts the ring on, his hand will turn to dust."

"Wow!" Kita's eyes became saucers.

Chapter 29
Amanda's Plan

"Dispose of this." Bayne closed the burner phone and tossed it to one of the guards.

Adrienne was starting to feel the strain in her neck. Keeping the blades from stabbing her was taking its toll. She didn't know if she could hold out for thirty-six hours. *If worse came to worse, I'll just lean my head, take off, and feel the pain when I come back. But I'm not giving in to this guy no matter what.*

Bayne stood in front of her and removed her gag.

"Now we'll see what kind of friends you have. My bet is they're foolish enough to think I'll actually let you go after I have the book. That's the thing about you 'honorable' types; too trusting."

Adrienne said nothing.

"For your sake, you better hope they come through sooner or rather than later. Thirty-six hours is a long time in the collar." Bayne retrieved his gold lighter, fired up a cigar, and left the room.

She looked directly at Wrancor who was still sitting on the sofa. "What is the longest you ever lasted?" Adrienne asked when Bayne had left.

"What do you mean?" he answered.

"I know this thing has been around your neck. What's the longest you ever held out?"

Colton looked at the two guards still at their posts. "Wouldn't know. I've never seen that thing until today. Looks like a real pain."

Adrienne studied his face. She knew he was lying. She gave him a knowing smile. "Whatever you say."

* * *

"Absolutely not!" Dr. Armitauge rose from his chair and waved his hands like an umpire at home-plate giving the safe call. Amanda had just finished detailing her plan. "Way too dangerous. I am not putting Kita in danger again and that's final."

"But Oliver will be with me and I won't actually go into the apartment," Kita pleaded.

"We won't know exactly what condition Adrienne will be in," said Amanda. "If she can't retrieve the ring, Kita will have to be there. We can't let Wrancor get it."

"What do you think, Francis?" Arthur looked over at his brother.

"I don't like the idea of letting Kita out of our sight. However, I think Amanda is right. I'll go along with it as long as Kita promises to not physically go into the apartment."

"I promise."

"It is a good plan, Dr. A," Oliver said. "I'll get Boyd and Malek up to speed when we're in the air. I'm having two men sent here from the Madison office with extra security just in case. They'll do a good job. We'll leave in one hour. I want time to spare."

"I'll have Gabriel get the schematics of the tower and forward them to you," Dr. Armitauge said.

Twenty hours later, in the black of night, they were on a beach in Altona Coastal Park, southwest of Melbourne. Oliver was strapping Kita to his para-gliding harness. She could hear the wing fluttering behind them when Oliver clipped his carabiner to the cable hook on the back of a jeep. He gave the signal and Boyd drove forward and Malek let out the cable. The wing filled with air and Kita felt the rush as they lifted off. They went higher and higher.

"How many feet of cable is he going to let out?"

"The tower is 980 feet tall. We're four miles out. With this breeze I figured about 100 feet of drop per mile. I padded that a bit. If I calculated our distance from the tower correctly we'll need almost 2000 feet of cable."

"How did you figure that out?"

"You've had Algebra, right?"

"Not yet," Kita said.

"Oh, well, it's right triangles. I can show you when we get back."

"That's okay. It sounds like something more up Amanda's alley."

Boyd gave the jeep's horn one short blast.

"That's our signal." Oliver reached in front of Kita and released the clip.

Kita tensed and squeezed Oliver's arm.

"Scared?"

"Are you sure about this?" Kita asked.

"No worries. I can land on a dime in a 15 mph wind. Putting us on top of the tower will be no problem."

There was no 15 mph wind that night, only a slight whispering breeze. The lights of the city reflected on the bay. It was hard to tell exactly where the city ended and the reflection began. Kita could feel the slight turns and dips as Oliver pulled on the guide wire handles; floating them over the city in a gentle descent. The night air was cool and Kita's skin was all goose bumps.

"It's right over there." Kita pointed to the tower straight ahead.

"Kind of hard to miss," Oliver quipped.

As the roof of the tower loomed closer and closer, Kita started to get nervous.

"Remember now, we are going to land on our feet and we may have to run at first. Try to stay upright. Ready?"

"I think so."

Suddenly, Oliver pulled on the handles with great force and they banked out of the way of a radio tower. He pulled sharply again and they slowed to an almost full stop. They hit. Kita tried running forward until she realized her feet were dangling a few inches off the ground. Oliver released the free line and the wing crumpled behind them. He quickly pivoted and pulled in all the guidelines. He stuffed the wing and the lines into a pack. He unhooked Kita from the harness and stepped out of his.

"I thought you said I'd have to run." Kita finished loosening her straps.

"If I had lost my balance you would have had to."

Oliver set the pack against the housing of a giant air conditioning unit. He pulled out his shoulder holster and slipped it on. Then he double-checked a gun strapped to one ankle and a blade strapped to the other.

"Now we wait."

"Do you want me to look quick and make sure she's there?"

"Just a glance and don't let that dog see you."

Kita laid her head against Oliver's chest and went out. She hovered down to the top edge of the window of Bayne's main room. She dipped her head and peeked. Adrienne was still in the armchair. She was still bound and the evil collar was still attached to her neck. Bayne and Wrancor were nowhere to be seen.

* * *

The Book of Ciphers and the ring had been carefully packaged in a sealed container and placed in a leather satchel. Amanda had picked out a flower shop in Hoppers Crossing less than three miles from the drop address. Boyd was there promptly when the doors opened for business.

"How may I help you this morning?" asked a boy in his late teens. He was standing behind a glass counter wearing a green uniformed shirt wrinkled enough to make one think he had slept in it. *Doogie*, was stitched in black thread above the pocket.

"I need this delivered to 12 Chisholm Place over in Werribee. I want a few of those dahlias to go with it. There is an extra $200.00 if you can have it there within an hour." Boyd set the satchel on the counter and he used his well-rehearsed Aussie accent.

"It's not drugs or anything, is it? I can't get caught with drugs, mate. I'm on probation and all."

"Nothing illegal, just a special history book."

"Why don't you take it there yourself?"

"Lot of questions, Doogie. Do you want the job or not?"

"Don't get flustered, mate. I only . . ."

"It's a long story. The professor at that residence knows me but I don't want him to know the book was ever in my possession." He opened his wallet and showed the kid a professionally faked ASIO ID card.

The teen straightened up and his eyes widened in surprise when he recognized the Australian Secret Intelligence Organization logo. "For real, mate?"

"For real," Boyd answered. "When they ask you, tell them it is a special delivery for Mr. Bayne."

The kid put his hat on, grabbed his keys, and scooped up the satchel. "It will be there in thirty minutes," he promised.

Boyd handed him $250.00. "This should cover it," he said.

"No wuckers!"

"Oh, and one more thing," Boyd added. "Someone will be close by."

A serious expression of realization swept over the lad's face.

When the kid hopped in the delivery van, Boyd sent a text: ON THE WAY

* * *

Malek was parked five houses down the lane from 12 Chisholm Place. He positioned the car for a perfect view of the front door through his side mirror. He was ready when a van with HCF on the side pulled into the dead end. A young kid stepped out holding the satchel and a small bouquet. He rang the doorbell.

Malek adjusted his ear bud. A small microphone transmitter was part of the satchel's buckle.

"Who are you, kid?" the man asked as he opened the door.

Malek recognized him. *Still not too bright*, he thought to himself.

"Delivery from Hoppers Crossing Floral."

"No one ordered anything from some floral place," he said.

"It's a special delivery for Mr. Bayne," Doogie said.

"Who sent you?" The man took the satchel from Doogie's hand and looked inside.

"Some guy from ASIO."

The man took out his phone and pressed once. "They used a flower delivery service . . . just some kid . . . it's been carefully packaged . . . I can do that."

He closed his phone and put it back in his coat pocket. "Here's the deal, mate. I don't have any money for a tip, so on your way."

Doogie didn't need to be told twice.

Malek pulled away from the curb and drove a few miles per hour below the speed limit down Ballan Road. Two minutes later he was passed by a speeding Range Rover.

PACKAGE IS IN TRANSIT, he texted.

That Amanda girl is pretty smart, Malek thought to himself.

Chapter 30

Recovery

Oliver and Kita slipped through a service door on the roof and crept down a flight of metal stairs. The entire 91st floor was an endless mechanical room. They camped out in a corner behind a massive boiler. It was too cool outside to remain on the roof. They ate dried cherries, roasted almonds, and dark chocolate. The schematics that Gabriel sent detailed the top four floors. The 90th was more mechanical and storage. The 89th had a commercial kitchen and a high-end restaurant. The 88th was a "pay to enter" observation venue. The 87th was Bayne's. However, there was a narrow staircase that went directly from the commercial kitchen to Bayne's kitchen. Oliver determined this would be his point of entry when the time came. For now, they waited.

Then the text from Malek came through.

"We're up girl," he said.

***

Adrienne was calling on every ounce of will power and strength to keep from going crazy. It had been over twenty hours in the collar and the back of her head and her neck were screaming in pain. She stared at Bayne with all-out hatred when he and Wrancor strolled into the room.

"Comfortable?" Bayne snickered. "Looks like your people decided to play the game. The book is on its way."

He opened a small case and removed a syringe. He secured a thick rubber band above her elbow and felt for a vein.

"I have found this little drug so very useful over the years. It is derived from an ugly shrub in the outback. I was taught how to use it by an aged Aborigine. You will be completely paralyzed, yet conscious. Can't give you too much or your heart will stop. Can't have that."

He injected the needle and pushed the plunger.

"Cerberus. Come. Sit." He pointed to a spot on the floor directly in front of Adrienne's chair.

The dog obeyed.

"Colton, maybe you can tell our guest what else this drug is good for."

Wrancor lowered his gaze before he spoke. "We tried it once when I was younger and I couldn't leave my body."

Bayne put all the tips back on the razor points of the torture collar and looked at Colton. "Just in case she can overcome what you couldn't. If she gets out, you follow her."

Adrienne could feel the drug start to work. It burned inside her and she panicked when she couldn't move her fingers. She realized she wouldn't be able to manipulate the ring. The only good thing, was it also deadened the pain in her neck.

* * *

Kita looked at Oliver as he read the text from Malek.

"They're in the elevator. We have to move," he said.

Kita laid on the floor in their little hiding corner and Oliver made his way down to the service entrance of Bayne's kitchen.

Kita hovered once again just above the window to Bayne's main room. When she saw how Cerberus was sitting, she had a more unique idea. She hovered in the space just above the ceiling so she was behind the dog whose attention was fixed on Adrienne. She poked just enough of her face through the ceiling panel so she could see what was going on. The dog never had a clue.

The elevator opened. It was the two men who had held Kita captive at the house. One of them handed the satchel over to Bayne.

"At least you can deliver a package without screwing up. Go out to the station and wait for further instructions"

Bayne opened the top flap of the satchel and carefully removed the sealed contents.

When Bayne set the satchel on his desk without examining it, Kita realized the men would be able to hear everything. Bayne hadn't discovered the listening device.

"Well now, let's see exactly what we have here."

He broke the seal and took out the book. He turned over the leather cover examining the first page and examined it for over a minute. Then he did the same thing to the next page.

"Looks like some sort of translation of a code. I think it's time for the ring."

Kita started looking at Adrienne a little closer and noticed she wasn't moving. She wasn't reacting to anything Bayne was doing. She wasn't even blinking. Kita wasn't sure what the problem was but she was worried.

Bayne pulled the little box out of the package and opened it. He held the ring close to his face and examined the markings. He looked at Adrienne.

"If that collar won't get you to do what I want, I have a feeling what I learn from this book might."

Kita wondered if she should command the ring to come to her right now. However, she remembered that Amanda was convinced

Adrienne wanted Bayne to put the ring on. So she waited.

Bayne slipped the ring onto the pinky of his left hand and turned back to the book. Nothing happened.

At first.

Suddenly, he screamed in horror. What used to be his hand was now a pile of blood-stained granules at his feet. The ring was in the pile. Bayne grabbed his wrist where his hand used to be and kept screaming. Miraculously, there was no more bleeding. Wrancor, the two strongmen, and Cerberus all snapped their attention to the bellowing tyrant.

Kita focused her attention on Adrienne but still no reaction.

"Kill her!" Bayne shouted, pointing to Adrienne.

Kita realized she had to act. She commanded the ring and it flew to her thumb. She fingered the lightning bolt and focused on Bayne's henchman. The guns melted in their hands. The metal in their phones melted. The watches on their wrists melted. They both yelled and ran to the kitchen. One started filling the sink and the other pulled ice trays from the freezer and dumped them in the sink. They both plunged their hands under the water trying desperately to put out the burning pain on their hands and wrists.

The whole time, Cerberus was barking at Kita like crazy.

"The other one is here. Get her, you imbecile!" Bayne shouted at Colton.

Kita focused on Bayne and fingered the bolt on the ring once again. His precious cigar lighter turned into molten gold right in his pocket. It started his pants on fire and burned a hole into his leg. His Rolex melted on his other wrist and his screaming reached hysterics until the gold fillings in his teeth melted. Then he crumpled to the floor and passed out.

When Kita turned around, Wrancor was waiting for her. She could see the hatred flaming in his burnt orange eyes. She was as disgusted as ever by his ugly green reptilian body. He flew at her and grabbed her around the throat with both hands.

"Bet you didn't know you could feel pain, did you? I told you I would end you, you little dill!"

Kita reached up and clasped Wrancor by the wrist. He became frozen. She removed his hands from her throat and kept a good hold on his wrist.

"Now who didn't see what coming?" she said.

She was surprised that while he was paralyzed he was also as light as a stick of balsa. She waved him around a few times and laughed until she realized she didn't know what to do with him next.

She heard Oliver and some commotion in the kitchen. She dragged Colton along to have a look. Oliver was standing next to the sink. The two guards were on the ground. Their hands and feet were zip-tied and they were still groaning in pain. Then Malek and Boyd came in through the servant entrance to the kitchen.

"Where's Kita?" asked Boyd.

"Her body is still lying under that blanket up by the boiler," Oliver said. "Go back up and stay with her."

Boyd sprinted back up the back staircase.

As Oliver ran into the main room, Malek followed. So did Kita, still dragging Wrancor behind her. Cerberus was now barking non-stop.

"Take that dog and lock him in a different room," Oliver commanded.

Malek grabbed Cerberus by the scruff of the neck and dragged him to a back bedroom and closed the door on him. Oliver studied Adrienne and he looked around for the ring.

"She's been drugged or something. Let's get her out of this collar."

Malek disconnected the battery just like he did with Kita. They both looked over at Wrancor's body lying on the sofa.

"What do you think?" Malek asked.

"Put it on him! Put it on Him!" Kita screamed, knowing full well she wouldn't be heard.

"I think we should see how he likes it. Put it on him," Oliver said.

Malek clamped the collar around Wrancor's neck, sat him up, and pulled off all the rubber tips. "What do we do now?"

"We wait," answered Oliver. "Hold his head up so he doesn't get all cut up."

"How long am I going to do that?"

"Let's give him a few minutes. If he's long gone, well that's just too bad for him. If he stayed close and Kita remembered her training, he's probably having the shock of his life right about now."

Kita pulled Wrancor over to the sofa. "You heard what they said. If I let go of you, you better go back to your body. If you take off, they're not going to hold your head forever. If you go back to your body, I'll make sure they take the collar off before we leave. If you attack me again, I'll just keep you out here until Mr. Malek there gets tired of holding your head up."

"Why would you make sure they take the collar off me when you leave?" Wrancor asked.

"One thing I've learned the last week is that nothing good comes from revenge."

"I don't trust you."

"I can't hold on forever. It's up to you."

"Okay, I won't attack."

"Promise me!" Kita demanded.

"Okay, okay, I promise."

She let go.

Wrancor hovered a few feet away from her. "This isn't over," he sneered.

"It is for now," Kita answered.

Wrancor went back into his body and shook his head. Malek let go.

"Colton Wrancor, I believe." Oliver moved next to the sofa.

"What's it to you?"

"You've seen what's happened. We've got what we came for. No need to get smart-mouthed," Oliver answered.

Wrancor didn't respond.

"Tell me what's wrong with Adrienne," Oliver continued.

"She's been drugged. It will wear off in a couple of hours."

Kita and Boyd walked into the room together.

"I promised him we would take that off before we left." Kita pointed to the collar.

"You did, did you?" Oliver said.

"Yes."

Oliver faced Wrancor. "Lucky for you, Kita has a heart."

"You know," Kita added. "Your guy is finished." She pointed to Bayne still passed out on the floor. "You could come with us."

Wrancor's answer was an ugly stare.

"Is the car ready to go?" Oliver asked.

"Ready," answered Boyd.

"Very well. Kita, bring the book and the satchel. Malek, you and I will carry Adrienne down to the parking garage. Boyd wait here until we call, then you can let him loose. Then catch a flight to Chicago and I'll contact you in a couple of days."

"Sounds good Boss."

Kita placed the Book of Ciphers back into the sealed compartment, slid it back in the satchel, and slung it over her shoulder.

Before they went to the elevator Kita remembered she had one more tidbit for Colton. "If you do anything to Mahshando, both Adrienne and I will be back for you. And we won't be nice. I promise."

"Who's Mahshando?" Wrancor asked.

"My friend, the silverback, you threatened to harm."

"No promises."

"I'll keep mine. You've seen what we can do."

An hour later, Kita, Oliver, Malek, and a still paralyzed Adrienne were airborne.

Oliver made his call.

"Why did you make him wait to release Wrancor?" Kita asked.

"Can't have him following us. He can never know where the island is."

Chapter 31
Apologies Accepted

The effects of the paralyzing drug wore off during the refueling stop in Hawaii. Kita and Oliver were walking on the tarmac, getting the kinks out from hours of being confined to the cabin. When Adrienne poked her head out the door. She held the railing on her way down the steps.

"Oliver," she called.

Oliver turned around but Kita ran to her and buried her head in Adrienne's embrace.

"I'm so sorry," Adrienne said. "This is all my fault."

"What do you mean?"

Adrienne explained about her carelessness at Ayers Rock and allowing herself to be captured.

"But that doesn't mean you have to apologize to me," Kita said.

"If they hadn't stumbled on to me, I doubt they ever would have thought to look for you."

"It doesn't matter," Kita said. "It's over."

Kita stood back a moment and studied Adrienne. Her astral body was so sleek and strong but her physical frame was far more frail than she expected it to be. Her hair color had washed out. Not her eyes though, they were clear and sharp. Kita could see a bit of the family resemblance, especially the fact that Adrienne was only an inch taller.

"I suppose this means I'm not going to get much taller."

"Probably not, my dear."

The rest of the plane ride, Kita told Adrienne about her parents, her brother Zach, her pets, all her adventures with Amanda, letting the animals loose at the zoo, her special friend Mahshando, and the Aegis Preserve. Adrienne loved every minute of it.

Francis, Arthur, and Amanda were waiting on the wharf when the boat pulled into the hidden cavern of Ile Brouillard. Barney and Goldie were there too, tails wagging.

Francis held Adrienne and would not let her go. Barney, Goldie, Amanda, and Kita were one big hugging, slobbering, messy jumble.

Arthur patted Oliver and Malek on their shoulders and told them, "Job well done men."

While Adrienne and Francis were still embraced, she lifted her head and looked at Arthur. "I'm so sorry."

"We will discuss those matters later. Let's enjoy the moment *mon precieux*."

Adrienne tapped Amanda on the shoulder. "So you're the one."

"The one?" Amanda asked.

"Oliver told me you figured out the meaning of my message. On top of that, do you realize there are trained analysts at the CIA and Homeland who could not devise a plan as well thought out and effective as yours? Even down to the detail that I might not be able to get to the ring. I am amazed. How old are you?"

"Fourteen."

"Brilliant."

Amanda got all red in the face and Kita smiled.

"I'm famished," stated Oliver.

"We thought you might be," Francis said. "Let's go upstairs."

Enrique had prepared a feast of grilled salmon, fresh asparagus, and butter creamed pasta with walnuts. There was a pineapple and raspberry dish, freshly baked bread, jams, and a platter full of assorted truffles. Barney and Goldie sat at Kita's feet and she made sure a steady stream of scraps made its way to the floor.

Kita looked at each person seated around the grand table. She realized she loved each one, which felt a bit weird for her. After all, except for Amanda, two weeks ago she didn't even know these people existed. Yet, somehow she felt she belonged to them and they belonged to her. And somewhere deep within her, a feeling she wouldn't have been able to put into words, she knew they would be part of each other in the future as well. She reached out and took Amanda's hand and Amanda squeezed back. Kita knew they would be linked together for the rest of their lives.

After dinner, they retired to the great room for blackberry gelato.

"Tomorrow will be a big day for you girls," Arthur announced.

"What do you mean?" Kita asked.

"You're going home. You still have two weeks of school left."

"School? I can't go back to school," protested Kita.

"You can and you must. Plus, your parents are expecting you."

"But I thought there was going to be training, and doing assignments, and stuff," said Kita. "A school here?"

"You will be back this summer," Arthur continued.

"But —" Kita looked over at Adrienne.

"I'm coming with," Adrienne said. "I want to introduce myself to your family. Besides, I can't let you out of my sight just yet."

* * *

Molly and Carter Griffith, Mike and Stacy Tenzio, and even Zach came running out of the house when Oliver pulled the Suburban into the Tenzio's driveway. There were hugs and kisses and laughing, and lots of oh my, oh my.

Except for Zach. "I'm glad they didn't kill you," was all he could muster.

Oliver and Adrienne stood off to the side. They were both grinning.

When it was time for introductions, Kita held Adrienne's hand as she brought her to her parents.

"Mom and Dad, this is Adrienne. She's my —" She stopped short as she thought about her other grandparents.

"It's okay Kita," Stacy said. "A girl can never have too many grandmas."

Adrienne held out her hand and Stacy clasped it with both of hers. They looked into each other's eyes with knowing smiles.

"Come in, come in." Stacy swung her arm in a wide invitation. "We've got Kita's favorite on the table."

"Pepperoni and green olives?"

"And thin crust," said Mike.

Oliver started walking back to the car.

"Aren't you going to join us?" Stacy asked.

"Thanks, but no. I have some unfinished business with a zoo administrator about a female elephant." He winked Kita's way.

Kita ran and hugged him. "Oliver, you're the greatest!"

* * *

Later that afternoon, Stacy, Mike, Kita, and Adrienne sat in the shade of the back patio eating raspberry ice cream.

"Adrienne?"

"Yes."

"Why didn't Dawn want me?" Kita asked.

"My relationship with Dawn was complicated. She resented me being gone a lot and she didn't like living on the island. Arthur and I were determined it would be safer for her if she didn't know what I was and what I could do. I believe she resented having part of me closed off to her. I sent her to live with Francis and Marie. She eventually got involved with a boy and got pregnant. Instead of letting us take care of her, she ran away. We put every resource we had to find her and we did. But she had already given birth and would tell us nothing."

"But why didn't she want me?"

"She was very sick when we found her. I think she loved you very much but knew that your only chance at a good life was away from her."

"Why didn't she stay with Francis and Marie?"

"I think she had completely surrendered to her addiction and knew they would make her stop using when they found out."

"But I was a normal baby, wasn't I?"

"Yes," Stacy broke in. "Now that I know the story, it is quite a miracle that you didn't have any bad effects from Dawn's drug use."

"Anything else?" Adrienne asked.

"Who's Dawn's father?"

"Maybe that is one of those things Arthur and I will help you understand this summer on the island."

"Kita. That's enough," Stacy said.

"It's all right," Adrienne said. "We'll talk about it this summer."

"Okay then," Kita said.

"Good. Then you and I have someone else we have to pay a visit to."

"Who?"

"You have a special friend that you need to talk to and so do I."

Kita's eyes brightened. "Oh yes, of course. Mom, we'll be right back."

Adrienne and Kita both laid back on the lounge and closed their eyes.

"Where have they gone off to?" asked Mike.

"The zoo," Stacy answered. She was smiling.

When Kita and Adrienne floated into Mahshando's house, he stood, beat his chest, and let out a roar that shook the glass. The bystanders all took a step back and pointed. Adrienne waved her hand and a frosty mist covered the glass. No one could see in.

"How did you do that?" asked Kita.

"There is much I have to teach you."

Adrienne turned to Mahshando. "I see you're smiling," she said.

"I'm happy."

"This is my grandma," Kita said. "Her name is Adrienne."

"I am Mahshando," he put his fist to his chest. "I am most pleased to meet the grandmother of my favorite human."

"The honor is all mine," Adrienne said.

"You only need to be here for a few more days," Kita interrupted. "A big truck is going to come and take you to the happy place I told you about."

"Are you coming with?"

"No. But I will be here to make sure it's done right. And I'll come and visit you. I promise."

"I believe your word," Mahshando assured her.

"Adrienne, can I borrow the ring for a second?" Kita asked.

Adrienne took the ring off and slipped it onto Kita's thumb. Kita hovered over to Mahshando and gave him a gigantic hug.

"You can feel me!?" Mahshando exclaimed.

"I love you," Kita told him.

Next, they went to visit Mtotah. She stood on her hind legs when she saw Kita and Adrienne hovering together.

"You found each other," she said.

"Yes, we did!"

Mtotah turned toward Adrienne. "You never came back."

"I know and I'm sorry and I have no excuse. Will you forgive me?"

"Even though we elephants have memories that are long and true, we also have forgiveness that is complete and total. I forgive you."

"Thank you," Adrienne said.

"We have some really good news," Kita said.

"Yes?"

"In just a few days a big truck is going to come and take you to a place where you can walk in one direction for miles before you have to turn around. You'll be able to take a bath in a lake and all the greens you can eat will be fresh and tasty."

"Where is such a place?"

"It will take three sunsets to get there but your trip will be safe."

"How come this is happening?"

Adrienne placed her arm around Kita's shoulder. "This girl Kita here has made some powerful friends the last couple of weeks and it's all her doing."

Mtotah slowly bowed down so her front knees were on the ground. "I am forever yours," she said.

Kita stroked her behind the ear. "And I am forever yours.

Chapter 32
The Send-Off

Monday morning came and so did the school bus.

"Wow! I've never seen you do lime green before," Kita said.

"I think this is going to be my color for the summer," Amanda answered.

"I like it."

Longstream and Warthog looked disappointed when the girls got on the bus.

"Oh man, I was hoping you two were kidnapped like they said on the news," Longstream complained.

"The news never said we were kidnapped," Amanda quipped. "They just speculated that two girls *had* been kidnapped. They never said who."

"The description sure sounded like you two," he said.

"I'm sorry, Ben. I probably used too big a word for you. S.P.E.C.U.L.A.T.E.D.," Amanda spelled it out. "It means they were guessing."

"I know what it means, lime ball."

"If you weren't kidnapped where were you all last week?" asked Warthog.

"Kita went to Australia twice and I hung out with a quantum physicist on a secret island."

"You're a riot," sneered Warthog.

"Say, Amanda, how do you suppose those four dogs knew about the cigarettes in Longstream's backpack?" asked Kita in a loud voice with a bit of a mocking tone.

"I'm not sure," Amanda answered. "But I am curious if those dogs will find out any other secrets he has."

A look of half confusion, half fear, twisted Longstreet's face. He looked like he had just bit down on something hard and bitter. And of course, he looked as oafish as ever.

When the girls sat down Kita had a new thought about Ben Longstreet. Two weeks ago, he was the biggest burr in her saddle; her sworn enemy. Now, she regarded him as a nuisance no more bothersome than a gnat. Next to Bayne and Wrancor, he was like a little boy who just graduated from diapers.

"I hope he tries to get rough with us next fall," Amanda whispered into Kita's ear.

"Why's that?"

"Oliver is going to teach us jujitsu this summer."

Kita grinned.

* * *

10:00 AM Saturday Kita and Amanda were in front of the cameras with April Hunnicut from Channel 7. The big day had arrived. A large, safari-brown semi-truck was parked behind them. In dark green letters, AEGIS PRESERVE arched over a mural of free-roaming animals that covered the length of the trailer.

When the red light turned on above the camera, April spoke into her microphone. "I'm here again this morning with Kita Tenzio and Amanda Griffith, the two girls who began the Free Elliot campaign. Tell us, girls. This must be an exciting day for you."

"Yes," Amanda began. "We want to thank all the people whose

contributions made this day possible. We're very pleased that Elliot and Wendy are going to be free."

"And what about you, Kita?" April Hunnicut held the microphone to Kita's face.

"I know Elliot is going to be thrilled that no one can stare at him anymore. I think Wendy will be especially happy to be able to roam as far as she wants. She won't have to go back and forth, back and forth."

"You talk as though you know what these animals are thinking," April said.

"It's just a feeling I have," answered Kita.

The cameras recorded both Mahshando and Mtotah walking into the back of the giant trailer. What the cameras couldn't record was Adrienne. She was walking next to each one, using her telepathic powers to soothe their minds, assuring them the end of this trip was going to be all that Kita had promised.

* * *

Colton Wrancor leaned back in the overstuffed chair that was planted in front of the large stone fireplace in the great room of Bayne's ranch house. He spread his feet toward the glowing logs and sipped his drink. He sat up when the doctor came back into the room.

"What's the verdict?"

"He'll live, I think. He'll need plastic surgery on his leg. I think the salve I put on his wrist will work. I instructed the nurses to reapply it every six hours. I'm going to keep him in a drug-induced coma for at least another week. I have no idea what to do with his mouth. I've never seen anything like it. I'll give you the name of a good oral surgeon I know. He needs to have it looked at right away."

"Anything else?" Colton asked.

"He should really be in a hospital."

"No hospitals."

"All right. I'll be back out here tomorrow to check on him. I know better than to ask, but what happened to his hand? It looks like it just disappeared."

"You're right, Doc. You know better than to ask."

When the doctor left, Wrancor went into Bayne's office. He swung open the Remington painting that was mounted on a hinged panel. He studied the door of the wall safe. Inside that safe was all of Bayne's secrets, the foundation of his empire. *There won't be any need for you, Claude, once I figure out how to get in there.*

Back at Ile Brouillard, deep in the terra cotta vault, in its airlocked case, the glowing light of the blue gem on the scroll of the ancient astrals, pulsed a little stronger.

About the Author

Jeff Hill lives in Minnesota... even in the winter. He enjoys spending time with family and friends, biking, fishing, hiking, vitamin D therapy, and exploring small towns.

He can be reached through his website: tryingtosee.com

Other books by Jeff Hill

Trying to See an Eclectic Devotional

The Wars of Bent Creek

Available @ Amazon Books or @ tryingtosee.com

Coming next from Northern Edge

JUSTICE

Made in the USA
Monee, IL
14 February 2023

27688328R00128